Aggie's
Anniversary

Aggie's
Anniversary

JAMES BARCLAY

LINDSAY PUBLICATIONS

First published in 2003 by
Lindsay Publications
Glasgow

ISBN 1 898169 30 6

British Library Cataloguing-in-Publication Data
A Catalogue record of this book is available
from the British Library

Designed and typeset by Eric Mitchell, Bishopbriggs, Glasgow
in Plantin 10 on 12 point
Cover illustration by John Gahagan, Glasgow

Printed and bound in Finland by WS Bookwell

CONTENTS

DEDICATION

To Maggie Dun and Bill Anderson
of the *Sunday Post*
who flung open wide the door

CHAPTER ONE

AGGIE'S BIG DAY HAD ALMOST ARRIVED. IT WAS THE DAY THAT Aggie Gallagher had planned and looked forward to for months – yes for years. She was determined that this celebration would be the one to end all celebrations. Her golden wedding shindig would be twenty-four carat. She and Harry had talked and planned it many times and now tomorrow was the big day and everything was prepared.

Harry would be delighted with the arrangements. The invitations were out and the catering organised. Her gastronomic choice would have him licking his lips. Her cheeks puffed up like an excited toad as she inflated the last balloon. Breathless, she flopped on to the easy chair and relaxed for a moment, recovering from her marathon blow out. She rose and fastened the red balloon to the stretched string across the living room and stood back and surveyed her work. She smiled. Yes, perfect, she thought. The red balloon was now in a line-up with its white, green, blue and yellow siblings and together catching the reflection of the light bulb, twinkled and winked like a maharanee's necklace in the slight breeze coming in from the half-open window of her Glasgow home in Bridgeton.

Directly above the sideboard where Aggie and Harry's monochrome framed wedding photo stood, was a banner of crepe paper stating in gold letters:

Happy Golden Wedding Anniversity to Aggie and Harry

Harry and Aggie always promised each other that their anniversary would be celebrated in style and now that it had arrived she was disappointed that it could not be celebrated in much better style. A hotel function room would have been more appropriate. But that takes money. She sighed. She would do her best.

The problem of the catering had been uppermost in Aggie's mind. But that had soon been resolved by a visit to Mr Patel in his corner shop where she purchased a batch of vindaloos. Aggie knew of Harry's love of India and that gave her a good idea of what to serve.

It all began when Harry served with the Royal Horse Dung Regiment – affectionately known as the Magnificent Crappers in Bombay. When he was demobbed and returned home he brought a little bit of India with him.

The telegram had merely said, 'Be hame on Friday.' No time was mentioned and an anxious Aggie had spent the day hingin' oot the windae' watchin' for him. Her heart leapt when she saw him marching round the corner, his kit bag slung over his shoulder and a wide grin on his face. Her eyes narrowed when she saw how he was dressed! It was the dead of winter and Harry was used to wearing his tropical uniform. He would catch his death of cold and people would be staring at him. Indian gear was all too well – but not in this climate. She ordered him to change his clothes immediately or people would think he was a nutcase. Reluctantly he agreed and discarded the purple sari and golden sandals and put on the tweed three-piece suit Aggie had purchased for him at Paddy's Market.

Things settled down and once more Harry got into the swing of things – boozing, punting and swearing at football matches.

Now Aggie was worried. She had posted out the invitations weeks ago and until now hadn't received any acceptances to join in the celebrations. Except from her sister Dolly in America and an ambiguous note from her brother Sammy. The thought of no one turning up was too much to bear. Harry had great confidence in her knowing her reputation for organisation.Her name came to the fore when she organised a Rangers Supporters' rally at Celtic Park. A large television screen was installed and the thousands of fans were stunned when it burst into life and the face of the Pope appeared hand-waving and smiling, saying 'Hail to the Rangers Supporters'.

The fans saw the Pope's expression change when a cleric whispered in his ear that there was no chance of hail falling on the assembly – or snow or rain for that matter.

Aggie's celebration just had to go well. She remembered how years ago she and Harry sat down over a glass of rich ruby wine and he took her hand in his and was emphatic that they would have a golden wedding to end all golden weddings – even if he had to pawn his Victoria Cross. He had won the coveted medal in Egypt in 1942. The bloke he won it from in a poker game took it badly and had kicked a camel.

Yes, Aggie wanted the celebration to go well as she never had the pleasure of celebrating her own parents' golden wedding anniversary. This was due to the fact that they never had one. Her mother had run away with a tattooist who had made a big impression on her.

Morning came, although still dark, as Nancy stirred the two cups of tea and called, 'Mammy, tea's ready.'

Aggie breezed into the room, did a twirl and said, 'Well, how dae Ah look?'

Aggie was dressed in a two-piece rust-coloured gaberdine suit-with a matching pill-box hat and a pink carnation pinned on to her lapel. Nancy stood, hands on hips and surveyed her mother not saying a word.

'Well?' Aggie said impatiently.

'Er –' Nancy stammered, 'dae ye no' think ye're a wee bit over the top, Mammy?'

Aggie's eyes narrowed. 'Ye know whit day this is, don't ye,' she snapped. 'And whit dae ye mean. *Over the top*?'

Nancy could have kicked herself. She had hurt her mother and she was sorry. She knew how her mother had been looking forward to this day. 'Ah'm sorry, Mammy,' she said, 'Ah didnae mean anythin'.'

'Well, if ye're referrin' tae ma apparel,' Aggie sniped, 'Ah'll tell ye somethin'. Ah am dressed the wey Ah want for to be dressed. It's yer faither Ah want tae please and he likes me in rust. And Ah want yer da' tae be proud o' me. It cost me a bomb and ye must admit, Nancy, there urnae very many wimmen in Glesva dolled up like me right noo, eh?' Aggie did another twirl.

'Aye, well, Ah'd agree wi' that,' Nancy said, 'Ah must admit ye might be right, there canny be many wimmin in Glesca dressed up as poshly as you right at this minute.'

'That's because the Barraland Belles are no more,' Aggie said, shaking her head sadly.

'It's because it's only six o'cloack in the mornin', Mammy,' Nancy retorted.

'Ah, but whut a moarnin',' Aggie said. ' Jist think it's fifty years ago the day that yer faither and me stood side-by-side in front o' the minister when yer da' proamised for tae love an' support me for the rest o' ma life.' There was pride in Aggie's voice.

'And so he did, Mammy, so he did.' Nancy was very fond of her father.

'Aye, though it was me that supported him maist o' the time,' Aggie said. 'Especially oan a Setturday night comin' up the stair.'

Nancy chuckled.

'Ye were awfu' fond o' yer da', wuren't ye, hen?' Aggie said.

'Oh, aye, Mammy,' Nancy said with a deep sigh.

'Remember when ye were a wee lassie he used tae tie up yer pigtails?' Aggie said.

Nancy grimaced. 'Oh, aye,' Nancy said, 'that was wan thing Ah didnae like him daein' tae me.'

'Maist wee lassies like their faither playin' wi' them an' tyin' up their pigtails,' Aggie said.

'No' tyin' them oan tae the pulley and then pullin' it up tae the ceilin', Mammy.' Nancy said.

'Ach that was jist his wey, hen,' Aggie said. 'He was jist showin' ye the Indian rope trick.'

'On a Setturday night ye could smell ma da' before ye saw him,' Nancy said, screwing up her nose.

'Aye, right enough,' Aggie said with a slight smile. 'The dug used tae dash under the bed when he came in.'

'That was because he used tae pick it up and make a fuss o' it,' Nancy said. 'Wee Bonzo didnae like that.'

'Ach there was nae herm in it,' Aggie said. 'It didnae dae the dug any herm, so it didnae.'

'Wan whifff o' ma Da's breath and that wee placid dug became a raging tyrant,' Nancy said.

'Ach, ye're exaggeratin',' Aggie said.

'Ah'm Ah,' Nancy retorted, 'Whit aboot the time, efter a close encounter wi' ma da', it dashed doon tae the street and knocked hell oot the coalman's hoarse.'

'Ach, away wi' ye,' Aggie said. Nobody, even Nancy, could ever say anything bad about her Harry – not that Nancy had anything but love for her dad.

'Well, Mammy,' Nancy said, 'ye're still goin' ahead wi' yer celebrations, eh?'

'Oh, aye,' Aggie said, 'we always proamised each other that we would celebrate this day in style.' She nodded towards the balloons. 'Yer da' appreciates a' this fuss. Ah know he does although he hisnae said anythin'.'

'And ye know why he hisnae said anythin', Mammy,' Nancy said.

'Why?' Aggie said, raising her brow.

''Cos he's been deid the last five years,' Nancy said.

'No' in here he's no',' Aggie said, pointing to her heart. 'Ah'm celebratin' oor life together. We had oor ups and down but every couple has them. But we did love each other. He's the only man Ah ever loved, besides the invitations are oot and although Ah've only had an acceptance frae oor Dolly, Ah'm a' excited, An' Dolly says she's bringin' a favourite of the silver screen alang wi' her – int that excitin'?'

'Oh, it is,' Nancy said. 'Imagine, ma Auntie Dolly, leavin' the tenements and goin' away tae Hollywood for to be a big film star. She must've had the bug since she was a wee lassie, eh?'

'We a' had, the bed was crawlin',' Aggie said. 'Ma maw had tae throw the mattress oot intae the midden.'

'Wis it that bad?' Nancy asked.

'Nancy, it walked doon the stairs itsel',' Aggie said.

'But it didnae stoap ma Auntie Dolly frae chasin' her dream?'

'While we wur bitten, Dolly wis smitten,' Aggie said.

Aggie was re-living those early days.

'Every Setturday efternoon we'd find her staunin' in the queue for the weans' matinee at the *Arcadia,* in London Road and when the doors opened, the screamin' and bawlin' could be heard at Glesca Cross. And oor Dolly was the first tae rush in and plant her erse on wan o' they widden seats, so she wis. She sat there, face fixed tae the screen and on the faces o' Betty Grable and Rita Hayworth an' that and from then on she was transported tae her dream world and there an' then she decided that she was gonny be a film star.'

Nancy sat with her mouth wide open as she soaked in the wonderful tale of her auntie's determination to escape from the tenement glaur to the cinema glamour.

'And she did,' Aggie went on, 'she became wan o' them – a thespian.'

'Och, ye've jist spoiled it, Mammy,' Nancy grumped. 'Whit you're sayin' is that ma auntie Dolly should really be ma uncle Dolly.'

'Naw, naw, hen,' Aggie said quickly, 'a thespian is an actor – somebody wi' greasepaint in their veins.'

'Auntie Dolly had greasepaint in her veins?' Nancy asked.

'Listen, when she got knocked doon wance and needed a transfusion, they didnae send tae the bloodbank for a supply, they sent tae Dulux,' Aggie said.

'Och, Mammy, there ye go again,' Nancy laughed. 'How did she get started on her road tae fame?'

'She went tae the Landressy Street library and sat there for 'oors studyin',' Aggie said.

'She was determined, eh?'

'She came in wan day an' said she was studyin' pose and Ah telt her she was daft. Ah mean we had them a' ower the hoose – wan under each bed, Ah didnae see whit good that was gonny dae her.'

'Ach, Mammy, she meant *poise*, a different thing altogether,' Nancy, hand on hip, marched up and down giving a demonstration.

Aggie blushed. 'Anywey,' she said, 'Dolly hitch-hiked tae Southampton and caught a tramp steamer goin' tae New York and it was on board that she met the man that wis gonny change her life forever.'

Nancy clasped her hands to her bosom. 'Oh. How romantic,' she cooed. 'Was he tall, dark and handsome and a millionaire?'

'It was a tramp steamer she was oan, Nancy, no' Onassis' yacht,' Aggie snapped. 'Naw, he was wee, had a postage-stamp moustache under his nose and wore a pair o' baggy pants.'

'She met *Charlie Chaplin*?' Nancy gushed.

'Naw, she met Adolph Hitler,' Aggie said.

'How did he chinge her life?' Nancy asked, puzzled.

'He broke her nose,' Aggie said, 'and through that Dolly got a job at Metro Goldwyn Mayer as an understudy.'

'Surely no' tae Betty Grable?' Nancy gasped.

'Tae Jack Palance,' Aggie said, adding, 'but it was a start. Her looks catapulted her right up the ladder and before long she was getting' star parts. They didnae have tae spend much on make-up, y'see.'

'Whit kinda parts did she get?' Nancy queried.

'Did ye ever see Fay Raye in the film *King Kong*?' Aggie asked.

'She was Fay Raye?' Nancy asked.

'She was *King Kong*!' Aggie said. 'Then came other starring roles in *Tarzan and the Lost City*.'

'Auntie Dolly played Jane?' Nancy cried.

'Cheeta, she played Cheeta,' Aggie said. 'Then came '*Lassie Come Home*, wi' Roddy McDowell.'

'Ah thought Elizabeth Taylor played opposite Roddy McDowall in that film?' Nancy said.

'Aye, she did,' Aggie said, 'Dolly played Lassie. But she *did* play opposite Roddy later on in *Planet o' the Apes*. And she did get rave notices when she was in *Antony and Cleopatra*, on Broadway,' she added.

'Wonderful!' Nancy said, 'A very demanding play.'

'Aye, the *New York Times* critic said she was the best Antony he had ever seen.'

Nancy laughed. 'Whit aboot ma uncle Sammy?'

'Ah, ma wee brother Sammy,' Aggie sighed. 'Sammy was the black sheep o' the family. He broke ma maw's heart when he ran away frae hame tae make his fortune.'

'Well, Ah think ma granny should've been proud o' her son wantin' tae escape frae the slums tae better himsel',' Nancy said. 'Whit age was he?'

'Four,' Aggie said.

'And did he make his fortune?'

'He became the godfather o' the Gallygate. Telt everybody he was in the mafia.'

'An' wis he?' Nancy asked.

'When anybody asked him who his family was he would snarl and say jist wan word – *mafia*.'

'Mafia?' Nancy repeated.

'Aye, mafia a family o' muggers – at least Ah think it was muggers he said.'

'Tell me somethin', Mammy,' Nancy said, 'just *how* did ma faither die?'

Aggie had never discussed Harry's death with Nancy or anybody else for that matter. She was too embarrassed. She would not even allow her daughter to view Harry in his big wooden box. Nancy could not understand her mother's reluctance to discuss her dad's demise or to allow her to see him in the horizontal position. She had seen him many times in that position.

Aggie ignored Nancy's inquiry and Nancy could see that, once again, she was wasting her time.

'It's jist too bad that ma da' isnae here for the celebrations, eh?' she said.

'Ah'm jist wonderin' if there's gonny be *anybody* here,' Aggie said dismally. 'Ah've got a' these vindaloos tae get rid o',' she added.

'And,' she went on, 'yer da' *will* be here – here in spirit – seventy proof if Ah know ma Harry. Besides, Ah proamised yer da' as he lay in his dyin' bed that Ah would celebrate this wonderful day and that's why he died wi' a smile oan his face.'

'Mammy,' Nancy said, ' he died wi' a smile oan his face because that wee blonde nurse put his teeth back in.'

Aggie flipped. 'Ur you suggestin' that your faither, ma Harry, was layin' there tryin' for tae impress that wee Marlyn Monroe look-a-like?'

Nancy shook her head. 'Naw, naw,' she said. 'but ye must admit ma da' did hiv an eye for the ladies.'

'Nonsense,' Aggie said.

'Mammy, remember wee Angus McSweeney who lived up number twinty-seven wi' yon big blonde an' her auld ninety-two year auld maw?'

'Whit aboot it?' Aggie said, looking quizzically at her daughter.

'Well,' Nancy said, 'Ah didnae want tae tell ye but Ah wance saw ma da' up the close wi' that wumman.'

'Wi' that big blonde?' Aggie said, drawing down her brows.

'Naw, wi' the auld maw,' Nancy said.

Aggie's muscles relaxed, 'Aye, well, the good man that yer faither was,' Aggie said, 'he probably thought that the poor auld sowel was lonely and was jist showin' her a wee bit affection.'

14

'He was definitely showin' her somethin',' Nancy said.

'Yer faither was a good man, he stood oot in the community,' Aggie said proudly.

'He stood oot right enough, but only when he was in the Orange Walk, Mammy,' Nancy said.

'Whit dae ye mean by that?' Aggie snapped.

'Mammy, ye don't walk doon the street in an Orange Walk wearin' a Celtic jersey,' Nancy said, shaking her head.

'It was the only warm jersey he had,' Aggie said, 'and there was nae bias in yer da.' Aggie sighed. 'Naw,' she went on, 'yer faither was a complete gentleman. He had a moustache and everyhin'.'

'Ah know ye loved him,' Nancy said.

'Frae the first minute Ah clapped ma eyes oan him, hen,' Aggie said. ''Ah'll never forget that night,' she went on, 'In Barraland, it wis. Ah was jist staunin' there when yer da' sauntered in – well, mair o' a swagger, really. Oor eyes met across a crowded room.'

'It sounds like he wis full o' himsel',' Nancy said.

'He was full o' somethin', that's for sure, 'Aggie said. 'Anywey, he swaggered ower, dressed tae the nineties, he was, in the latest Teddy Boy suit. Ah jist stood there, mesmerised, and suddenly found masel' playin' wi' his big, furry ears. Teddy boy suits wur a' the rage but yer faither always had for tae go wan better. He was a Yogi Bear look-a-like. Anywey, oor eyes met and he said, 'Ur ye dancin'? Well, seein' Ah was staunin' quite still Ah couldnae very well say Ah wis, but before Ah could say anythin'. He had me oan the flair.'

'Oh, how romantic,' Nancy said. 'Whit did ye dae?'

'Ah got up, dusted masel' doon and we moved intae Jitterbug Coarner,' Aggie said.

'An' that's when love struck. Eh?' Nancy said.

'Ah knew there was somethin' different aboot him right away.' Aggie said.

'Whit was it, Mammy?'

'His smile,' Aggie said.

'A flash of pearl, eh?' Nancy sighed.

'Naw, he had nae teeth in, anywey, efter that came the winchin' and we eventually got married. Ah'll never forget that wonderful honeymoon. Ah always loved Millport.'

15

'Did ma da' enjoy yer time together in Millport?'

'He went tae Las Vagas – he likes a wee gamble y'see,' Aggie said. 'Ah didnae mind,' she added.

'Was he good tae ye, ma da'?' Nancy said.

'Aye, well like a' merried couples we had oor wee differences, especially oor first couple o' years,' Aggie said. 'Although he gied me everythin' durin' that time – maistly the boak. But he was the love o' ma life and a wee boak noo and then did nae herm. We prayed for a family and then wee Rosie came alang and then you.'

'Wee Rosie?' Nancy wondered why her mother rarely mentioned Wee Rosie.

'Aye, Wee Rosie,' Aggie said, 'yer da' was very religious and prayed for a wee lassie who had the cream complexion of Shirley Temple.'

'An' did Wee Rosie have the complexion of Shirley Temple?' Nancy asked.

'Mair like a Mormon Temple,' Aggie said. 'Like red brick, it was. When yer faither saw her he accused me of hivin' an affair.'

Nancy knew this was impossible. *Her* mother would never be unfaithful to *her* father.

'Who did he think you had an affair wi'?' she asked.

'Geronimo,' Aggie said.

Nancy burst out laughing. 'Ach, away wi' ye,' she chuckled, nudging her mother with her elbow. Then, thinking of Wee Rosie, she said, 'Ye never really ever telt me whit happened tae Wee Rosie, Mammy.'

Aggie shook her head sadly. 'We loast her when she was two,' she said, dabbing her eye.

'Whit a shame!' Nancy said. 'Whit did she die of?'

'Oh, she didnae die.' Aggie said, 'It was wan Setturday we wur in Lewis's, in Argyle Street, when Ah took ma eye aff her for jist a minute and she wandered aff – and we loast her. We never saw her again.'

'That is dreadful!' Nancy said.

'Ah was devastated but yer da' was quite pleased,' Aggie said. 'He still swore she was the daughter of Geronimo.'

'That's terrible,' Nancy said. 'Ma wee sister vanishes and naebody cared.'

'Naw, naw,' Aggie protested, 'Ah cared. She was ma wee lassie even though she wis the ugliest wean ye ever saw.'

'She couldnae hiv been *that* ugly,' Nancy said, 'Ah mean, you an' ma' da' wurnae bad lookin'.'

'Believe me, Nancy, she *wis* ugly. She wis a Miss Piggy look-a-like.'

'Ah canny believe that,' Nancy said.

'Nancy,' Aggie went on. 'Ah was invited tae Esther Goldberg's son's weddin' in the synagogue and Ah took wee Rosie wi' me and they widnae let us in.'

'Ah canny believe ma faither couldnae love wan o' his ain,' Nancy said.

'Believe me, hen, it was that rid face that did it,' Aggie said.

'Whit a terrible indictment!' Nancy said, shaking her head.

'Well, yer da' knew a' aboot indictments,' Aggie said, 'had a few himsel'.'

'Ur you sayin' ma da' was well known tae the polis?' Nancy said in unbelief.

'Nancy,' Aggie said, 'wan day yer da' went intae Tobago Street polis oaffice tae ask directions and got six months.'

Nancy believed none of this and decided to change the subject. 'Goin' back tae ma Auntie Dolly,' she said, 'if she was *that* ugly how come she didnae dae somethin' aboot it?'

'But she did,' Aggie said, 'she decided for tae visit wan o'them cosmoponic surgeons.'

'Cosmetic surgeon, ye mean,'Nancy corrected.

'Aye wan o' them,' Aggie said.

'She got some plastic surgery, then, eh?'

'She had mair plastic than a giant Leggo set. Hen,' Aggie said. 'We wur always frightened for her tae sit too near the fire in case her face would melt and tae make matters worse, Ah think the doactor that operated oan her was an apprentice. Ye should've seen her nose.'

'Was it too big?' Nancy asked.

'It was right under her left ear,' Aggie said.

Nancy went into convulsions. She shook her head. Her mother was incorrigible. 'Ah'm away intae ma room, Mammy, an' put some claeths oan before yer guests start tae arrive,' she said.

'Time enough, hen,' Aggie said, 'Ah'm no expectin' anybody before four o'cloack. It's still the moarnin'.'

'But if Auntie Dolly's comin' a' the wey frae Hollywood, ye jist don't know whit time her plane gets in,' Nancy said.

'True enough,' Aggie said.

Nancy vanished into her room. Aggie's eyes fell on her wedding photo on the sideboard and a smile crossed her face. Taking the picture, she stood it on the table and sat down, cupping her face in her hands. Kissing Harry's smiling face, she sighed.

'Aw. Harry.' She began, 'here we are ma son, oor Golden Weddin' Anniversary fifty years, eh? Who would've thought. But Harry, you're no' here tae haud ma haun' or raise a gless, But we had some good years together. Never wance did ye lift yer hauns tae me – always used yer feet – but only when ye had yer slippers oan. Mind when we first met in Barraland and when we got merried. You wur daein' yer national service at the time. Ah was that proud o' ye. Ye wur waitin' for me as Ah walked doon the aisle. You staunin' there in yer general's uniform, me in ma white weddin' dress. A loat o' folk said you had nae right wearin' that general's uniform. In fact some even said Ah had nae right wearin' that white weddin' dress.

'We had oor ups an' doons jist like any other couple, Harry. You said things tae me that ye didnae mean. Things like, "Ah'll gie ye yer wages every Friday withoot fail." Ah said things tae you that Ah knew would hurt ye – like, "Ah thought yer maw was very mannish lookin." But ye had tae admit, Harry, that there wisnae many weans in the street whose maw got employed as Fraser's Santy Claus every Christmas.

'Aye, Ah loved ye, Harry, and still dae. Ye said ye'd be here and would make this a day for to remember. But ye're no' here, son, but ye're still wi' me right here,' Aggie pointed to her heart and sighed.

She had organised the whole *do* herself and was sure Harry would approve.

'Mr Patel, owner of the mini-supermarket, had welcomed her with a grin that would have done justice to an Osmond line-up.

'Ah, Mrs Goollagher,' he beamed, the light flashing off his teeth and blinding her momentarily.

18

'Is it that time already?' he inquired, having been forewarned of the impending golden celebrations.

'Aye, it is, Mr Patel,' Aggie said, smiling.

'So you wull be wanting your order for the big shindoog, aye?' Mr Patel asked.

'Aye, it is that,' Aggie said happily.

'Ah hiv your order a' ready,' he said, producing a large cardboard box from under the counter and placing it on top. Aggie sniffed in the strong smell of vindaloo curry. Aye, Harry would approve, she thought.

'You ur expecting many guests, Mrs Goollagher, eh?' the man said, noting the weight of the box.

'Stacks,' Aggie said, 'A' ma freens – and even ma sister, Dolly, frae Hollywood,' she said, with pride in her voice.

Mr Patel threw up his arms.

'Ah!' he cried, 'your sister, Dilly, is a member of the Scoattish Parliament?'

'Hollywood,' Mr Patel, 'no' Holyrood,' Aggie corrected. 'Although they're a' actors the gether, uren't they?'

Mr Patel laughed. 'Ah, your sister, Dilly. Is a film star, eh?'

'Hiv ye ever heard of the *It* girl?' Aggie asked.

Mr Patel's jaw dropped open.

'She was in that?' he stammered.

'Well, in a wey,' Aggie said, 'Did ye ever see a picture called 'It Came from Outer Space?'

Mr Patel nodded. 'Ah did – Ah did,' he said.

'Well, she was *It*,' Aggie said.

Mr Patel showed his teeth again.

'Your *Golden* wedding anniversary, you say, Mrs Gooleghar?' Mr Patel said.

'Aye, and wi' these vindaloos there's gonny be a hot time in the old town tonight,' Aggie said with a laugh.

Mr Patel was suitably impressed. '*Golden*?' he repeated.

'Twinty-four carat, son.' Aggie said.

Mr Patel clicked his tongue and pushed the box over the counter. 'It's a long time – one hundred years,' he said.

'*Fifty years*,' Aggie corrected. 'Ah know ma face looks like it's been well lived in – but it's no a hotel.'

Mr Patel showed his teeth again. 'We sell very good extra-strong mints if yer party should feel a wee bit stinko – know whit Ah mean?'

'Harry loved the smell o' curry,' Aggie said, 'and Ah am sure naebody wull complain.'

With a cheery wave, Aggie left the shop. She found the box of vindaloos getting heavier as she headed for the bus stop and was glad to rest it on the pavement and join the small queue.

The bus came within minutes and Aggie heaved and stumbled slightly as she lifted up her box of goodies.

The Pakistani bus driver noticed her plight and immediately jumped out and, taking the box, lifted it easily and placed it on the luggage platform. Then, turning to Aggie, gently took hold of her elbow and steered her to her seat.

'There ye are, hen,' he said and, noting the contents of the box, took an exaggerated sniff and said, 'Keep wan o' them for me, hen.'

Aggie had laughed, leaned back and relaxed glad that things had gone so well. As she approached her stop, Aggie rose and stood beside her precious cargo. The stop was just twenty yards from her two-in-the block house.

'This yer stop, hen?' the driver asked.

'Aye, Ah live just up there,' Aggie had said, pointing to her house.

'Right!' the driver said and, running past the stop, pulled up right outside Aggie's door. He took her by the arm and steadied her as she stepped off the bus. Taking hold of the box, he carried it up the path behind Aggie who fumbled for her keys. Putting the box on top of the kitchen table, he patted her shoulder.

'Have a rerr terr, missus,' and climbing back into the driving seat he was met by a round of applause by his passengers who had witnessed the whole episode.

Mr Patel had been very helpful and, looking inside the box, Aggie noted he had added some pompadoms 'on the house'. What a kind man she thought.

No further acceptances had arrived for Aggie's celebration. Here she was at *the* day with only a load of 'rubbish' mail put through her door that morning.

Aggie was beginning to get worried. Harry would not be pleased either. She had enjoyed her wee 'blether' with Harry and after returning him to the sideboard, let her eyes sweep round the room. There was an eerie silence with only a slight noise from the lightly swaying motion of the balloons due to the half-open window. Aggie walked through to the front door and raised the doormat to make sure no accepted invitations had accidentally been kicked underneath. It was daylight now and Aggie could see a touch of frost on the windscreens of the cars parked out in the street. She turned and closed the windows in the living room and checked that the central heating was fully on.

She was glad she had Nancy who was a blessing. She would never be alone as long as Nancy was there – until her daughter found herself a husband, that is. Then Aggie would have grandchildren. She might have had them now, she thought, if Wee Rosie had not wandered off. She wondered if Rosie was a wife and mother. Maybe Aggie was a granny already. She would never know.

Nancy had Harry's eyes. Yes, Nancy was cockeyed. Harry had one blue and one brown eye and sometimes he arrived home with a black eye. That was times when, standing at the bar, he would inadvertently lift the drink of the bloke standing next to him.

Aggie had likened her golden wedding celebrations to Queen Elizabeth's Golden Jubilee celebrations. After all she had been crowned a few times by Harry – specially on a Friday night when he staggered in with a broken pay packet and was met by a tirade from Aggie's well-honed tongue. Yes, the Queen and she were related through drink.

Being in the Orange Order, Harry was a great Loyalist and loved nothing better than participating in street parties, where he could sing at the top of his voice and show off his prowess in Highland Dancing. These street parties had Harry's adrenalin pumping at full force although often he was the only celebrant.

Aggie looked up as Nancy entered the room brushing her hair.

'Did Ah hear the post earlier?' she asked.

Aggie nodded, 'Aye', she said.

'Nothin'?' Nancy asked. She didn't have to wait for an answer. She saw the deep disappointment in her mother's face.

'Jist a letter tellin' me Ah'm in the final draw of the *Reader's Digest's* Prize Draw,' Aggie said.

'Never mind, somethin' will turn up,' Nancy said, giving her mother a peck on the cheek.

'Nancy,' Aggie said, 'when Ah look intae yer eyes ye remind me o' that famous song, so ye dae.'

'Whit song's that, Mammy?' Nancy said, her brows going up.

'Ye're a cockeyed optimist,' Aggie said.

Nancy laughed. 'Everythin' will be a'right, you'll see,' she said, 'Besides, you said ma da' said he would take care of everythin' – no matter what.'

'Aye, well he didnae know he wis gonny snuff it, did he? Bloody inconsiderate o' him. So it wis.' Aggie screwed up her nose.

'Talkin' aboot ma daddy, ye never *did* tell me how he died,' Nancy said, knitting her brows and hoping for the truth this time.

'It's too embarrassin', hen,' Aggie said.

'Ah'm auld enough noo, Mammy,' Nancy said.

'Ah couldnae bear thinkin' aboot it, Nancy, so Ah couldnae,' Aggie said, dabbing her eye.

'Did he no' hiv an inklin' that he was gonny snuff it so suddenly?' Nancy asked, putting a comforting arm around her mother's shoulder.

'Naw, in fact he'd started readin' *Gone With The Wind*,' Aggie aid. 'Noo, anybody that starts readin' that has got nae intentions o' snuffin' it.'

'Unless he didnae like it.' Nancy said.

'Oh, he liked it a'right.' Aggie said. 'He'd started callin' me Scarlett.'

'Did ye no' mind?' Nancy said.

'Ah didnae mind that so much but he started callin' the hoose Tara and even put a big oak sign outside the door wi' Tara burned intae it,' Aggie said.

'So, whit's wrang wi' that?' Nancy said, approvingly.

'In a single-end, three up?' Aggie snorted.

'Well, anyway,' Nancy said with slight impatience, 'ye hivnae telt me how he died? Ah'm a big lassie noo, Mammy. It must've been a real shock tae you when he passed on so suddenly.'

'That's true,' Aggie said.

'That it was a big shock tae ye?' Nancy said.

'Noo, that ye're a big lassie – an' Ah hope ye don't get any bigger. Ye used tae be able tae come in that door sideways.'

'Nancy ignored her mother's remark.

'So ur ye gonny tell me?' she said.

'A'right, ' Aggie said, 'But ye're no' gonny like it.'

'Try me,' Nancy said. 'Was it the drink? Did ma da' take a good drink?'

'Did yer da' take a drink?' Aggie threw up her arms. 'That's like askin' if John Wayne could ride a hoarse.'

'Well?' Nancy pressed,

'Yer faither wance got a joab fillin' up barrels in a brewery and they went bankrupt within' months o' him startin'.'

'So it *was* the drink that sent him intae eternity?' Nancy said. Aggie shook her head. 'Naw, it wisnae, hen,' she said.

'Whit wis it then?' Nancy said, raising her voice.

'Well, Ah never, ever wanted for tae tell ye, Nancy,' Aggie said, 'it broke ma heart.'

'Mammy, if you don't tell me right this minute, you ur gonny be left on yer own for to celebrate,' Nancy was losing her rag.

'Ah think Ah'm gonny be on ma own anyway,' Aggie said sadly.

'*Mammy*!' Nancy cried.

'A' right, a' right,' Aggie said. 'It wis self-inflicted. Yer da' committed suicide. There, ur ye satisfied?'

Nancy was silent – stunned. 'Bu . . . bu . . .' she stammered.

'A drug overdoze,' Aggie went on, knowing Nancy's next question.

'A drug overdoze?' It hadn't sunk in. 'Whi . . . whi . . .whit wis it – cocaine – heroin – ?' she said the words almost in a whisper.

'Nane o' them,' Aggie said

'So whit wis it he took an overdoze of?' Nancy almost yelled.

'Viagra,' Aggie said.

'*Viagra*!!' Nancy cried.

'Viagra,' Aggie repeated.

'Geez, that must've been embarrassin' when the ambulance cam for tae take him tae the hospital?' Nancy said.

'He resembled a bell-tent when they cerried him doon the stairs,' Aggie said.

'How embarrassin',' was all Nancy could say.

'It was mair embarrassin' when we got him hame and the undertaker came oot,' Aggie said.

'How wis that?' Nancy asked.

'He couldnae get the coaffin' lid tae fit oan,' Aggie said. 'And when the undertaker produced a knife Ah put ma foot down. Ma Harry lived like a man and he's gonny get cremated like a man, Ah said.'

'Quite right, Mammy,' Nancy agreed, 'so, whit did youse dae?'

'The undertaker bored a hole on the lid and we got the card-boad bit oot of a toilet roll and yer faither bein' the good Royalist that he wis, we stuck a union jack on toap – and yer da' vanished through them crematorium curtains wi' the flag flyin' and the organ playin' *Roll Out the Barrel*.'

Nancy had to hide a smile.

'Well, then,' Aggie said, glad at last to get that off her chest. Nancy had to know sometime and that was it over. 'Time's getting'oan hen and Ah've got a stack o' vindaloos in there jist waitin' for mooths.'

'It's early enough yet, Mammy,' Nancy said.

'Ah wonder if Wee Alice McGeachie wull turn up?' Aggie said.

Wee Alice was Aggie's Best Maid at her wedding and lived across the landing of their tenement home.

Aggie thought of Wee Alice with affection. They were school-girls together although they did go to different denomination schools. They were the best of pals. Aggie thought of how they played together sitting on the hard, cold steps up the close, play-ing at 'shops' with clay shaped into all sorts of things – even money. Of how, on their 'mischief' days, they would tie together two doorknobs at opposite sides of the stair landing, kick each door and run away giggling and leaving irate tenants tugging at their doors trying to open them before realising that those 'wee tinkers' had been up to their old tricks again.

She remembered how they used to play at bouncing ball from between their legs against a wall and that reminded Aggie of Wee Alice's diminutive father who used to come home every Saturday night, sit on the bottom stair up the close and sing *Nellie Dean* at the top of his drunken voice and of her large, bullish mother who used to come charging down the stairs and bounce *him* off the wall.

Alice was a Catholic but there was no bigotry up the close. Everybody helped out everyone else be it financially or illness. When Aggie's dad was out of work and asked Wee Alice's dad for a loan so that he could buy a new 'tin-flute', he received the cash no bother, Alice's dad assuming that Aggie's old man was set for a job interview was surprised to see him playing his new tin flute during a practice Orange walk down Bernard Street. Alice's old man would have laughed that day if her mother had allowed him to put his teeth in.

Aggie had lost contact with Wee Alice. She had run away with a 'midgie' man and it was the 'talk of the steamie'. The friends hadn't seen each other for years and it was a mere fluke that Aggie spotted her old friend one day when she switched on the television set. Folk had always thought that Wee Alice, despite her size, could become a super model – even a film star. She *did* model garden gnomes for a while in London, while her lover, who deserted her within days of arriving there, was picked up by police for busking and causing a riot.

The London bobbies are usually tolerant of buskers but it transpired that he did his busking act an, Al Jolson impersonation, outside the offices of the British National Party.

'It was jist by luck Ah spotted Wee Alice on the television,' she said.

'Whit programme was that, then?' Nancy asked.

'It was wan o' they look-a-like programmes,' Aggie said. 'You know – folk who looked like famous people – Elton John, Johanna Lumley an' that.'

'Who did Wee Alice look like?' Nancy said.

'Charles Bronson,' Aggie said.

'If she looked like Charles Bronson how did ye know it was Wee Alice?' Nancy quite rightly observed.

'She was wearin' the same big brass earing she always wore. Ah recognised it 'cos it was me that gave it tae her,' Aggie said.

'Loats o' lassies wear big brass earings,' Nancy said.

'No' through their nose they don't,' Aggie said.

Nancy smiled. 'Ach, Ah think ye're haverin',' she said. 'She's probably jist a bit craggy wi' age now we a' get auld, y'know.'

'Yer faither didnae,' Aggie said sadly.

'Here, c'mon let's hiv a wee dram,' Nancy said, taking a bottle of *Bells* whisky from the sideboard and pouring out two glasses.

'Tae ma da',' Nancy said, raising her glass.

'Tae ma Harry,' Aggie said, raising her glass. 'Fifty years on – mind oor weddin' night, Harry?'

Aggie's eyes took on a dreamy look.

'Dae you remember yer weddin' night, Mammy,' Nancy said.

'Dae Ah remember oor weddin' night or do Ah remember ma weddin' night?' Aggie cooed.

'Dae ye?' Nancy repeated.

'Oh, aye, Ah remember it well, hen,' she said dreamily. 'Wee Susie Sweeney gave us the use o' her hoose that night. Straight frae oor reception in the Tent Hall, in Steele Street, we went, straight tae Wee Susie's hoose in Claythorn Street – a wee single-end it was. But it wis awfu' good o' her.' Aggie sighed.

'Aye, here's no' many would help ye oot like that nooadays,' Nancy said.

'Ah but we wur a' freens in they days, hen,' Aggie said. 'Susie had eight weans y'know. Yer faither and me wur exhausted when we got intae bed that night but the weans wur helluva noisy.'

'A' eight o' them?' Nancy said.

'The hale squad, ' Aggie said. 'Yer da' an' me had the bed recess but the weans had tae share the Morris Chair. But we tried for tae ignore them. We had a great day. Everything had gone well. The minister wis sober and everybody said Wee Alice looked a picture – a picture of Dorian Grey, whoever that wumman wis.'

'It's sad, though, int it,' Nancy said, 'You hivin for tae celebrate yer anniversary wi' ma da' no' here.'

'Yer da' *is* here,' Aggie snapped.'

'Dae ye think he'll be in heaven?' Nancy said.

'He'll be an angel, noo, although he'll no' need wings. He wis always fleein' without them when he wis doon here,' Aggie said.

'You've never really had any sadness in yer life, Nancy, hiv ye? She went on, 'Except maybe for that time yer faither wis readin' a magazine that had an advert sayin' "Hiv teeth like the Bee Gees," and he sent away for a set for your birthday – remember?'

Nancy grimaced and nodded. 'Ah was never so embarrassed,' she said.

'Ah know for weeks ye hated tae smile they wur that big. Mind the day he sent ye doon tae Ladbrooks for tae put oan his line and the man behind the counter wanted tae enter you in the St Ledger?'

'Aye, Ah ran oot the shoap,' Nancy said, her mind going back.

'Galloped mair like it,' Aggie said. 'Mind ye, up till then ye would never eat yer breakfast. Efter yer new teeth arrived ye insisted on porridge oats every mornin.'

'Millions o' people eat porridge oats for their breakfast every moarnin',' Nancy snapped.

'No' oot a hessian bag tied roon their neck, they don't,' Aggie said.

Nancy smiled. 'Aye, that wis a big mistake, so it wis, Ah wish ma da' had never picked up that magazine,' she said.

'Aye. He mis-read it,' Aggie said. 'It didnae say "Hiv teeth like the Bee Gees" it said, "Hiv teeth like the Gee Gees" – Ah but Ah miss him, hen. We went through life haun-in-haun. Ah even held on tae his haun as we walked doon the street. Ah had tae they wur everywhere. And we gathered a loat o' freens on oor journey through life – but where are they noo that Ah need them?' Aggie shook her head. 'Only yer Auntie Dolly has replied tae ma invitation – and she's tae come a' the wey frae America.'

'Did ye put R.S.V.P. on yer invitations?' Nancy asked

'Ah didnae spill wan drap when Ah was writin' them oot, hen, not wan drap,' Aggie said

'Aye, well there's time enough yet,' Nancy said, looking out the window.

'If naebody turn up for to help me celebrate this golden day Ah will hiv failed in ma journey alang the avenue of life, so Ah will,' Aggie said. 'The measure of yer life comes wi' the number o' freens you hiv gethered' she went on, sinking deeper into nostalgia. 'Real freens come tae comfort ye in times of sadness and grief and tae celebrate wi' ye in times o' joy and happiness. This is a bitter-sweet day for me, so it is. Not wan o' ma so-called freens – ach, don't get me started,' Aggie was hurt. She took a deep breath. 'Still, thank God Ah've got you, hen,' she said, squeezing

Nancy's arm, 'and yer faither might no' be here in the physical sense but he *is* here in spirit. Anythin' tae dae wi' spirit and he'll be there.'

She rose, walked to the door and stepped outside. She shivered as the cold air stabbed her. She peered up and down the street looking for any sign of life. First to the left and then to the right – nothing. Not even a prowling stray cat. Not one single meow to break the silence.

'Come in, Mammy,' Nancy cried, 'ye'll catch yer death o' cauld.'

Aggie closed the door and shuddered. She flopped on to the easy chair and gratefully accepted the glass of Drambuie Nancy handed to her. She sipped the drink and smacked her lips as the warm liquid wrapped itself around her stomach.

'No' even a shadow oot there,' she said with a sigh.

Nancy pecked her mother's cheek. 'Don't worry,' she whispered.

'Ah think Ah'll stick ma heid in the oven and die slowly,' Aggie said.

'Don't talk daft,' Nancy said, 'how wull ye dae that?'

'Ah'll set it at Gas Mark Two,' Aggie said.

Nancy's hand came up to her mouth as she stifled a chuckle.

A loud rapping at the door made them both jump.

'Don't tell me!' Aggie said.

'Ah'll get it,' Nancy said and hurried to answer.

Aggie poured another drink and swallowed it quickly and, gasping as it caught her throat, clasped her chest and flopped on to the chair. Her ears were primed and she could hear Nancy's voice talking to someone in the hall. Aggie's hand came up to her cheek.

'Oh!' she cried excitedly. 'It's Sammy.' It had been a long time since she heard that deep, rasping voice.

Nancy entered the room accompanied by a two-foot long cigarette holder, attached to the mouth of a fashionably dressed lady wearing a large, wide-brimmed hat.

'It's ma Auntie Dolly, mammy,' Nancy said excitedly.

'Dahling,' Dolly said, crossing the room and delicately planting a kiss on Aggie's cheek.

Aggie took a step back and surveyed this apparition who blew out a raging fog of grey smoke. 'Is that really you, Dolly?' Aggie said, drawing down her brows.

'In the flesh, Dahling,' Dolly said in deep baritone. Dolly carried what looked like a metal vase with an ornamental lid which she placed on the sideboard.

It suddenly struck Aggie that Dolly had come. She clapped her hands gleefully.

'Ye came Dolly, ye came!' Aggie cried.

'It nearly caused a fight with the studio, but I'm here, back in dear old Scatland.' Dolly said with a heavy American accent.

'Mr Spielberg was furious that I left in the middle of my picture,' Dolly said. 'But I threatened to go to Warner's if there was any argument.'

'Aye, Ah've left the Arcadia many a time in the middle o' wan o' your pictures,' Aggie said.

Dolly ignored the crack.

'Here, hiv a drink,' Aggie said, pouring out a large Drambuie.'

Dolly raised her hand. 'I only drink champagne, Dahling,' she said.

Aggie pointed to the two-foot cigarette holder.

'Ur ye tryin' for tae get away frae smokin'?' she said.

'Oh, very witty, Dahling,' Dolly said, taking another long drag.

Aggie rose and went to the door, Opening it widely, she stuck oot her head and looked around. Returning to the company she said.

'Ah thought you said yer wur bringin' a famous film star wi' ye, Dolly? It's no' Tom Cruise or John Travolta, is it?'

'No, no, Dahling,' Dolly said, ' it's him, 'She nodded towards the vase on the sideboard.

''If it's no' Tom Cruise it must be Tom Thumb?' Aggie said.

'*That*,' Dolly said seriously, 'is the ashes of the great Lassie.'

'Whit lassie's that, then?' Aggie asked.

'The great canine actress – or I should really say *actor* for the real Lassie was really a male.'

'Ye mean the wan we saw wi' Roddy McDowall was a boy dug in drag?'

Dolly nodded.

'A Gay dog, eh?' Aggie chuckled.

29

'Lassie's owner wanted him to be scattered in Scatland. The beautiful dog loved the Scottish accent even it was only Edmund Gwenn's.' Dolly said.

'Loved Scotland, eh?' Aggie said with a touch of pride.

'His owner did not want him to have any offspring and told him so. And he saw the disappointment in his very intelligent face. To soften the blow he told him he was taking him to be dressed and that bucked him no end. Lassie thought he was going to get kitted out in a kilt and sporran and he was completely shocked when he saw what they did to him.' Dolly said. 'His estimation of Scotsmen rose dramatically when he saw what they had to go through to allow them to wear the kilt.'

'A likely story,' Aggie said. 'But why ur ye hivin' tae scatter his ashes here, in Scotland?'

'It stands to reason,' Dolly said. 'His love of Scatland and, when his owner heard I was coming over here, he asked me if I would bring him with me and scatter him in God's own country.'

'Ah don't think they'll allow ye tae scatter them in Ibrox Park,' Aggie said.

'I was thinking more of Loch Lomond,' Dolly said.

'Well, Ah think ye should scatter them outside the Masonic Hall, in Whitevale Street, ' Aggie volunteered.

'Why there?' Dolly asked.

'It's obvious, intit. That dug wis a freemason.'

'You're talking rubbish, Dahling,' Dolly said. 'What makes you think that?'

'Ye canny tell me that *that* dug wisnae a mason. Ah saw it shake hauns wi' Roddy McDowall in *Lassie Come Hame*.'

'Don't talk nonsense,' Dolly snapped. 'The wee dug – dog merely shook its paw.'

'Aye, it wis the shake o' the paw a'right but only efter it rolled up the fur oan its left leg – ye canny tell me,' Aggie was adamant.

'Ah've never heard such tripe,' Dolly said, her accent slipping.

'Ye must've when ye read some o' the scripts they gave ye,' Aggie said.

'I'll lay poor Lassie on the Campsie Hills,' Dolly said with a finality.

'There's been a few lassies laid there,' Aggie said. 'Come tae think of it, you should be ashamed o' yersel' sayin' ye wur comin' here wi' a famous film star. And ye turn up wi' a deid dug.'

'It was an errand of mercy,' Dolly said.

Nancy diplomatically interrupted this dialogue.

'Ur ye sure ye don't want a wee drink, auntie Dolly?'

Dolly shook her head.

'No thank you, Dahling,' she said, 'As I said, I only drink champagne – Dom Perignon, to be exact.'

'The nearest we've got tae that is Dom Estos,' Aggie said. 'It gies ye a sparkle, right enough.'

'But I did sparkle, Dahling,' Dolly said, 'did you see my last picture?'

Aggie nodded.

'Ah'm gled,' she said.

'Gle . . . er . . . glad of what?' Dolly said.

'It was yer last picture,' Aggie said.

'You mean you didn't like my performance?' Dolly said with a hurt expression.

'The dug in that urn is, at this minute, gein' a better performance,' Aggie said facetiously, 'Although, Ah *wull* admit, they *did* make ye up for to look like the great Crawford.'

'I wasn't supposed to look like Joan Crawford,' Dolly said.

'Ah meant Broderick Crawford,' Aggie said.

'You always were a bit jealous of me, Aggie,' Dolly said.

'Jealous?' Aggie snapped, 'Ur you kiddin'? Ah didnae want for tae go away tae America and get kissed and slobbered a' ower by a' they men – men like Clark Gable an' Robert Taylor an' Brad Pitt an' that – yeuch!' Aggie shuddered.

Dolly's eyes scanned the room.

'Yes, I can see you wouldn't want to leave all this,' she said sarcastically, 'the Barras, the Sarry Heid, Ibrox an' that.'

'Glesca' a' chinged since you left, Dolly,' Aggie said, standing up for her home town.

'There's nae mair queuein' up oan the stairheid for the lavvy. 'Cos nearly everybody's got their ain, private lavvies – and, besides, there's no' many stairheids anyway. And there's mair smoke comin' frae your gub than ye'll see comin' frae a lum in Glesca – we've even got television and micro-wave ovens. You'd

31

be surprised how much we've chinged.'

Aggie was on her high horse – but it was all talk, Dolly was her sister and blood *is* thicker than water. She *did* admire her wee sister for going after what she wanted. Perhaps there was a touch – just a wee touch – of jealousy there. But not enough to count.

'Ach, but ye wur quite right tae get away frae it a'.' Aggie admitted. 'Tae get intae the world and chase ycr dream.'

'Everybody should chase their dreams,' Dolly said. 'Go for their ambitions. You never chased your dream, did you Aggie?'

Aggie laughed. 'Ah did – and Ah caught him,' she said.

'Not much of a dream, was it?' Dolly said, screwing up her nose.

'Whit dae ye mean,' Aggie snapped, flames coming from her eyes.

'Well, look about you,' Dolly said, 'a life in squalid little houses, waiting every Friday night for a drunken husband coming home from work with a grubby little brown poke containing his weeks's wages.'

'Well, that's where you ur wrang,' Aggie said. 'Ma Harry used tae come in every *Thursday* night, so there.'

'His wages intact?' Dolly said flatly.

'Aye, always,' Aggie said proudly, 'except for wan night he came in stinkin'. He'd loast his wages in an accident.'

'Drunk?' Dolly said.

'Naw, he explained that he had fell and his pey poke had fell doon a stank and he had spent 'oors tryin' for tae get it oot and that's the reason he was stinkin'. Them stanks are awfu' smelly ye know.'

'The whole story stinks,' Dolly said.

Nancy decided to leave the room in case they came to blows.

'See ye later, Auntie Dolly,' she said leaving.

'Yes, Dahling,' Dolly said, blowing her a kiss.

'Right noo,' Aggie said, hands on hips and steam jetting from both ears. 'Whit dae ye mean "squalid little hooses"?'

'Well, you must admit things could've been better,' Dolly said.

'Ur you forgettin' that oor maw brought us weans up in a wee single-end, *Dahling* – you, me, ma da', oor Sammy and a battalion o' mice that came oot every night.'

'That was in another lifetime,' Dolly said, beginning to feel sorry she had brought the whole subject up.

'Listen, Dolly,' Aggie said, 'we dae a' try tae better oorsel's. Some of us make it and some of us don't. You probably live in a "Des-Res" as they say nooadays?'

'I live in Bel-Air, in L.A.', Dolly said proudly.

'You live oan Hoat Air, Dolly,' Aggie said.

'I was glad to follow my dream and escape from my slum environment,' Dolly said, adding, 'you should be proud of me.' Dolly was hurt at her sister's outburst.

Aggie gave a long sigh. 'Aye, Ah suppose so,' she said, cooling down. 'Ah *am* proud o' ye, hen, make no mistake aboot that. Ah'm jist happy that this is ma golden weddin' anniversary and sorry that Harry's no' here tae share it wi' me – and you're the only wan that's turned up.'

Dolly pecked Aggie on the cheek.

'Happy anniversary, dahling,' she said. 'I may be a famous film star, Aggie, but, more important this day, I'm still your wee sister.'

Aggie felt better. Dolly strolled over to the sideboard and took up the old wedding photograph once more.

'A fine looking man, your Harry,' she said.

'Aye, a good worker and a canny man was ma Harry,' Aggie said.

'Canny? You mean he was shrewd with his money?' Dolly said.

'Naw, canny like, in for instance, it didnae matter whit Ah asked him tae dae roon' the hoose, he'd say, "Ah Canny".'

Aggie and Dolly's eyes met and they burst out laughing.

'Aye, but we had a good marriage,' Aggie said, a gleam in her eye. 'He loved me and that's a' that mattered. It was touch and go at the beginning, mind ye ,' she went on.

'Oh, how's that, dear?' Dolly said.

'Ah remember wan night, before we got merried, we were staunin' winchin' up oor close – we steyed three up. Mind?'

Dolly nodded. She well remembered.

'Well, we wur staunin' at the back o' the close and Harry took the fag oot his mooth. Took me in his erms, gave me wan o' his chips and said, 'Wan day, hen, Ah wull buy you a wee bungalow wi' a white-picket fence roon' it and stacks o' flooers in the gairden' – he was right generous that wey, ma Harry wis.'

'And did he ever?' Dolly said slightly mockingly.

'Naw, he had nae money,' Aggie said. 'But he *did* gie me a wee single-end and a windae boax.'

'What else do you remember of that night?' Dolly, being the romantic that she, and all showbizzy folk, are.

'Ah remember his vinegary kisses,' Aggie said.

They both burst out laughing once more.

'Aye, ah kid on a loat aboot Harry,' Aggie said, 'he might only hiv been five-feet four but he was a giant of a man in ma eyes. He's probably lookin' doon oan us right noo and hivin' a good laugh.'

'Ye don't think he's changed, then?' Dolly said.

'Oh, he's chinged a'right,' Aggie said.

'In what way,do you think?' Dolly said.

'Well, he's deid for a start,' Aggie said.

'I always think that one's first love is the greatest of all,' Dolly said with a sigh.

'Oh, Ah wisnae Harry's first love.' Aggie said, 'he was goin' wi' a wee Irish wumman when he met me. She wis a communist and, he said, while staunin' up her close a' she would talk aboot wis steam engines an' platelayin' and things like that. He didnae ever leave that close wi' romance in his heid – but he knew how tae drive the four o'cloack train frae Central Station tae Euston.'

'What was this Irish woman's name?' Dolly asked.

'Harry called her "Red Biddy",' Aggie said.

'Appropriate!' Dolly said.

'Harry said it wis because o' her that he began tae take a good, stiff drink,' Aggie said. 'And that was a loat tae blame for the wey he became.'

'Drunk?! Dolly volunteered.

'A *Stiff*!' Aggie said.

'Oh, you poor dear!' Dolly said.

'Naw, no'poor, hen,' Aggie said, 'skint sometimes maybe, but never poor. Ah widnae hiv traded ma Harry for a' they glamour boys in Hollywood – although, Ah must admit that Ah envy you getting' kissed by stars like Clark Gable an' that. He wis ma favourite efter A saw him in *Gone Wi' The Wind*. Puts me in mind o' Harry, that.'

'Clark Gable puts you in mind of Harry?' Dolly said with surprise.

'Naw, the wind,' Aggie said.

'It's a myth,' Dolly said. 'Kissin' Clark Gable was not all that it was cracked up to be. It's common knowledge that he suffered from halitosis.'

'Ah didnae want tae kiss his feet,' Aggie snapped.

'Halitosis, Aggie is bad breath,' Dolly explained.

'Oh!' Aggie blushed. 'Ah thought 'tosis' wis . . .'

'I know what you thought, Dahling,' Dolly interrupted.

'Bad breath can be a terrible thing,' Aggie said, making a face. 'Ma Harry suffered wi' it at times. Ah remember wance an auld wumman in his work collapsed and Harry gave her the kiss of life.'

'And saved her?' Dolly inquired.

'Naw, she died,' Aggie said. 'They held a post-mortem and had tae scratch their heids, when they found that she had died o' alcohol poisonin' — especially when she was president o' the Temperance Movement.'

Dolly pointed to Aggie's wedding photograph.

'Your Harry had a good head of hair, eh?' she said.

Aggie nodded.

'Aye, in they days he had that much hair they didnae call him Harry, they called him Hairy. But his lovely daurk hair a' started fightin' wi' each other.'

'What do you mean?' Dolly said,

'They a' fell oot. Aye poor Harry, his hair wis his pride an' joy. He had real thick, thick hair so he had. He washed it constantly but never used a shampoo. He always used a *real* poo. But it made nae difference. His maw wis manky and Harry wis forever getting sent hame frae school wi' a note frae the teacher sayin' she'd hiv tae dae somethin' aboot it.'

'No wonder!' Dolly said, 'I remember in school in those days, the doctor came round and examined our heads with a fine tooth comb.'

'Aye, well loats o' folk always said Harry needed his heid

examined,' Aggie said. 'But the crunch came wan day when, efter the doactor had been, Harry's maw got a note frae the teacher sayin' efter examinin' Harry's heid they didnae find lice – they found mice.'

'Did the doctor prescribe anything to alleviate Harry's problem?' Dolly asked.

'Aye, he suggested hivin' a moosetrap fitted,' Aggie said.

Another bout of loud laughter.

'Oh, Aggie,' Dolly said, 'you're better than Lucille Ball.'

'Wish Ah had her money,' Aggie said.

'I think it's marvellous you celebrating your Golden Wedding,' Dolly said in praise. 'I never, ever made an anniversary with any of my husbands.'

'How many did ye hiv?' Aggie asked, adding, 'Ah remember readin' that you had a perennial bouquet attached tae an elastic band so that when ye chucked it ower yer shooder tae a' they gigglin' auld maids dyin' tae catch it, it snapped right back intae yer erms.'

'Not true,' Dolly said. 'I just never met the right man.'

'Is it because ye're butch?' Aggie said.

'I am not butch,' Dolly snapped. 'I have a sore throat.'

'Ur ye sure you ur no' wan o' them?' Aggie said. 'Ah mean, remember when we wur wee lassies and like a' wee lassies, we liked tae dress up in oor maw's claeths and stoat aboot in her high heels?'

'Yes, I remember,' Dolly said.

'You dressed up in ma da's claeths and clumped aboot in his tackety-boots. Ah mean that should've gied ye an idea that there wis somethin' wrang,' Aggie said.

'Ach, it was just a whim,' Dolly said, dismissively.

'Ye didnae hiv tae smoke his pipe as well,' Aggie said.

Dolly shrugged.

'How many times were ye married anyway?' Aggie said.

Dolly placed her forefinger on her cheek. 'Let me see,' she said. 'Oh, yes, nine or ten times, I think,' she said.

'Geez, Dolly,' Aggie said, 'you make Elizabeth Taylor look like the Virgin Queen.'

Dolly ignored the remark. Walking over to the wall mirror, she stood gazing. Her hand came up to her cheek.

'Oh, God, Aggie!,' she exclaimed, 'look at me – do you think I'm getting old looking? I'm developing bags under my gorgeous eyes.'

'Mair like trunks, hen,' Aggie cruelly said.

'Looks are everything in America,' Dolly said.'It's the beautiful people who receive all the invitations. I was actually invited to the White House to perform before the president.'

'Which wan – George Washington?' Aggie said facetiously.

'Och, stop it, Aggie,' Dolly scolded. 'I performed for President Clinton.'

'A loat o' lassies did,' Aggie said.

'He was a perfect gentleman,' Dolly said, 'and very astute, too. As they say in the Glasgow patois, "There was nae flies oan him".' Dolly had fallen into her native accent no bother.

'That's because he didnae need them,' Aggie said, 'Never had time tae use them.'

Dolly quickly changed the subject.

'I thought you would have held your celebrations in a proper hall,' she said.

'Couldnae afford it,' Aggie said. 'Ah *did* try tae hire the Orange Hall but they've hired it oot tae the Union of Catholic Mothers for their Bingo night, so they hiv.' A bit of disappointment crept into Aggie's tone.

Dolly's eyes went to the ceiling. Aggie was incorrigible. 'Tell me about Harry's demise,' she said suddenly.

Aggie looked up quickly. 'Whit dae ye want tae know aboot them for?' she cried.

'About his demise – his passing away?' Dolly said, wondering what Aggie was on about.

'Oh, his *demise*!' Aggie said, 'Ah – er – thought ye said his denims!'

'I was stunned when I got your telegram,' Dolly said.

'Ye'll hiv tae watch yer drinkin', hen,' Aggie said.

'What's that got to with anything?' Dolly said, 'I said I was stunned when I received your telegram.'

'Oh, Ah thought ye said *stoned*,' Aggie said.

'So, how did he die?' Dolly pressed.

'Ah'd rather no' say, it's too embarrassin',' Aggie said.

'He didn't let you down at the end, did he? ' Dolly said. 'I mean, he died with dignity – he died with his head held high, eh?'

'No'only his heid,' Aggie said.

'Don't tell me if you don't want to,' Dolly said, seeing Aggie's anguish.

'I'm only sorry I didn't make his funeral. I was making a film – Crocodile Dundee.'

'Wur you the crocodile?' Aggie said.

Dolly laughed loudly. 'No, I had two very small parts,' she said.

'Ye always had,' Aggie said, 'till you saw that cosmoponic surgeon.'

'Everything went well, I take it?' Dolly said

'It was a lovely send-off,' Aggie said. 'The undertaker gave us a great coaffin deal – buy wan, get wan free.'

'Very quaint!' Dolly said.

'Aye, Nancy uses the other wan as a windae boax,' Aggie said with enthusiasm 'When people in the street pass by they cross themsel's. It's a great shape for growin' marras.'

Dolly could only admire Aggie. She was still in her environment and obviously had had a very happy life with her Harry. In a way Dolly envied her big sister.

'You know, Aggie,' Dolly said. 'in many ways I envy you. I thought that I'd have to get out to find my dream, that there was no other way. And I did go and I did find it. But you stayed put and you found yours.'

'Aye, right enough,' Aggie said. 'Folk are apt tae forget that it's no' where ye live or how ye wur brought up that counts. It's whit ye make o' yersel'. Ah mean, look at the famous people that came frae the slums – you for a start.'

Dolly hung her head in mock embarrassment.

'Then we had some members of the Scottish Parliament – though they don't really count – we had great men like William Shakespeare who came frae the Calton, Winston Churchill, who was born in the Gallygate and whose faither was a bookie up ma auntie Annie's close. We had oor great sportsmen, tae. Pele, the greatest fitba' player in the word, whose real name wis Shug Mc Sorley, came frae Barrafield Street.'

'Are you sure Laurence Olivier didn't come from McBeth Street?' Dolly said sarcastically.

'Aye, come tae think of it, Ah think he did,' Aggie said, then, 'or was it London Road? – disnae matter.'

Dolly found it hard to keep a straight face.

'Look, hen, ye must be starvin', sit there, ye're in for a treat.'

'Thanks Dahling,' Dolly said. She leaned back and took a long drag at her cigarette as Aggie hurried into the kitchen, returning within minutes with a plateful of steaming vindaloo. She planted it down in front of her sister with a flourish.

'There ye ur, hen,' she said with pride, 'get that doon ye.'

Dolly sniffed the delicacy and contemptuously pushed the plate away from her.

'I couldn't possibly eat that, Aggie,' she said screwing up her nose.

'Besides,' she added, 'I have a very important interview at the BBC and must go.' Dolly rose, surveyed her self in the wall mirror and headed for the door. Turning, she said, 'I really couldn't eat that hot curry and stand just inches away from the producer with a breath that would knock him down flat, could I?'

'Yer hali . . . hali . . . hallelujah ye mean?' Aggie said.

'Exactly,' Dolly said. 'I'm sure you understand.'

'Ah thought ye came here for to celebrate ma golden weddin' anniversary,' Aggie said with some bitterness.

'And so I did,' Dolly said, 'but when the BBC heard I was coming home they immediately jumped at the chance of considering me for a new soap they are contemplating. I'm just sorry I won't be here tae take part in your happiness. You *do* understand, don't you?'

Aggie's heart slumped. 'Oh, aye,' she said, 'Ah understaun'. Business always comes first, eh? Disnae matter aboot feelings so it disnae. Away ye go.'

Dolly stepped through the door only to be stopped in her tracks by Aggie yelling.

'Here, jist a minute, dahling, Ye might no' have won the Oscar but ye *hiv* won somethin' that is jist as coveted – the *ashes – here.*' Aggie thrust the urn into her sister's arms, waved a goodbye and slammed the door shut.

'That's me – a'hert,' Aggie said, turning and flopping into the chair.

Nancy came hurrying into the room. 'Did Ah hear the door shuttin'?' she asked, her eyes sweeping the room. 'Is Auntie Dolly away?'

'Aye, away wi' the fairies,' Aggie said, 'She didnae come ower here for tae celebrate wi me at a'. She had an appointment wi' the BBC. They want her for a new programme – probably makin' another series wi David Attenborough.'

Seeing the disappointment in her mother's face, Nancy poured another whisky and handed to her, saying, 'Here, Mammy, get that doon ye and relax. She's no' the only wan.'

Aggie thanked her daughter and took large gulp.

'Ah'm that worried, Nancy,' Aggie said, 'Yer faither wull be mad if naebody turns up – and so wull Ah. Who's gonny eat a' they curries?'

'Is that really whit's troublin' ye, Mammy?' Nancy said.

Aggie took another swig of the *amber nectar*, coughed slightly, and said, 'Nancy, yer faither wull turn in his urn if naebody turns up. He'll feel it's a slight on him and besides, Ah canny be expected for to eat two dozen vindaloos masel'. For a start the plumbin in this hoose leaves a loat tae be desired.'

'Ye're worryin' for nuthin', Mammy,' Nancy said reassuringly.

'Aye, well Ah don't know,' Aggie said, unconvinced. 'Where's wee Alice? No' a cheep frae her. Maybe she canny write. Maybe she sent an E-Mail and Ah never received it. A' the time Ah hear aboot these E-Mails and how marvellous they ur. So whit's so good aboot them when ye don't get them?'

'Ye need a computer, Mammy,' Nancy said.

'Aw, Ah thought thar E meant Eager – jist a fast movin' postman who loved his joab,' Aggie said.

Aggie had just stopped talking when there was a loud and frenzied rapping on the door. Aggie almost jumped out of her skin.

'Who the hell could that be?' she cried.

Nancy hurried to the door and there was inaudible talk coming from the lobby. Seconds later Nancy entered the room accompanied by a diminutive woman who had a worried expression on her face. Aggie jumped up.

'*Alice*!' she cried, sweeping the wee woman into her arms and squeezing her tightly. 'It *is* you, Alice, int it?' Aggie said with delight, 'and no' Charles Bronson. Eh?'

Wee Alice stammered but the words would not come out.

'Here, hen, sit doon,' Aggie said, guiding her to a chair. Nancy placed a large glass of whisky in her hand.

'Here,' she said, 'get that doon ye.'

Wee Alice took it in one gulp.

'Whit's the matter, hen, whit is it?' Aggie said with concern.

'Ah – Ah – Ah wis stalked by a man a' the wey frae the bus station,' Alice said, shaking.

'Wur ye frightened his dug might attack ye?' Aggie said.

'Whit dug?' Alice said.

'His guide dug,' Aggie said.

'He didnae hiv a dug,' Alice snapped, 'and besides, Ah am nut frightened of dugs. We had a dug for years but we had tae get it put doon.'

'Put doon where?' Aggie asked.

'Tae sleep,' Alice said, dabbing her eye. 'It took distemper.'

'Wan coat or two?' Aggie asked, adding, 'Ah know the feelin' Ah used tae hiv sleep problems.'

'Because o' yer dug?' Alice asked.

'Naw, because o' Harry.' Aggie said, 'He widnae let me get any.'

'Anywey, it's nice for to be here,' Alice said, 'Ah got a surprise when the television company forwarded yer letter tae me. Is it really fifty years since that day Ah walked doon the aisle wearin' that lovely froak?'

'Aye, Ah'll never forget it seeein' you walkin' doon that aisle. Ah was fair embarrassed, so Ah wis.'

'How did Ah embarrass ye?' Alice said with concern,

'Two things,' Aggie said, 'First, ye took yer joab too faur. We a' knew ye wur an usherette in the Arcadia but ye didnae hiv for to walk doon the aisle *backwards*.'

'And whit wis the other thing that embarrassed ye?' Alice asked, puzzled.

'Ye wur telt for tae walk doon at ma back cairryin' a posy, Alice – no' a po'

'Oh, did Ah dae that?' Alice said with a look of innocence.

'Ah widnae hiv minded so much if it had been empty.' Aggie said.

'It was jist rice, Aggie, for tae throw ower ye,' Alice said in way of anapology.

'Ah wis hopin' it was jist rice, Alice,' Aggie said.

'Ah wis that pleased for to get yer invitation, so Ah wis,' Alice said, smiling. 'And when Ah woke up this moarnin' and saw the lovely blue sky Ah immediately thought aboot your Harry.'

'It reminded ye o' his blue eyes, did it?' Aggie said with pride.

'Naw, his Rangers jersey,' Alice said. 'He always wore that Rangers jersey, so he did – never a suit.'

'Oh, that's no true.' Aggie said. 'He did wance get a suit – a light fawn, it wis – beautiful.'

'That would gie your eyes a rest frae Rangers, then, eh?' Alice said.

'It did – until he turned roon. Oan his jaicket was emblazoned *McEwans*!'

Aggie sighed. 'Aye, Harry was a Rangers fanatic. That was the sponsors at that time. On his death bed he made me promise that Ah'd bury him in a fitba' strip.'

'His beloved Rangers jersey?' Alice said.

'Naw, a Celtic strip,' Aggie said. 'He said he'd rather hiv wan o' them buried. Harry was always thoughtful that wey.'

Aggie's mind went back to their younger days when Harry would take her to Ibrox. Aggie would complain that she was famished and Harry assured her that he'd buy her a pie and a cup of Bovril. But he never did. When she complained he told her that a pie and a cuppa Bovril 'Isnae good enough for you,' and that he would treat her to a good square meal. And so she ended up with a Lorne sausage sandwich she downed with a cup of Oxo.

Aye, they were great days! she thought, looking back. Harry had settled down to married life and had taken up sport. He became a golfing fanatic. Where the word 'links' had once meant sausages to him it now meant *golf!*

Aggie was surprised how much Wee Alice had changed in fifty years. From a Charlotte Bronte look-a-like to a Charles Bronson look-a-like was no mean feat. But, still. Alice had turned up and that was just fine with Aggie.

Alice sat sipping the newly poured drink given to her by Nancy and she thought of happier times.

'Ah'll never forget your weddin' day Aggie,' Alice said. 'It was the very first time Ah had oan a lovely pink froak so it wis.' She sighed at the thought.

'It was the first time ye wore a lovely *clean* froak,' Aggie said. 'They used tae call ye "Gallus Alice" the lass wi' the manky hanky, the froak that gave ye the boak.'

'That was because ma maw ran oot on us weans. She took a powder and abandoned us,' Alice said sadly.

'Aye, well it wisnae Persil she took, that's for sure,' Aggie said. 'Ah don't think she ever heard o' the stuff. Clatty Mattie, they called her. Yer faither's dungarees used tae walk tae his work hauf an oor before he did.'

But this was all in another life. Alice would always remember Aggie as the friend who had brought a little glamour into her life, even it was for just one day.

'That *was* a lovely froak, Aggie,' Alice said, the picture of that day flashing into her mind. 'Did ye get it in the C&A?'

'Naw, the P.M?.' Aggie said.

'Prime Models?' Alice asked.

'Paddy's Market,' Aggie said without expression.

''Ah felt like a queen walkin doon that aisle. That lovely long froak right doon that ma ankles.' Alice sighed once more.

'Aye, but yer froak should have started at yer shooders, Alice, no' yer waist.' Aggie said.

'You had a loat of style in them days, Aggie,' Alice said. 'A' ra fellas were efter you. Remember yon big hunk frae Dalmarnock Road – the wan that looked like Victor Mature?'

'Aw, aye, Ah remember him,' Aggie said, screwing up her nose. 'He had a big tip for himself. Ah went oot wi' him for a while but always thought there was somethin' no' right aboot him. And then wan night he telt me he was goin' in for a transplant and Ah knew that was it.' Aggie shook her head.

'Shame!' Wee Alice said, 'He looked that healthy, tae. Whit wis it . . . Kidney, Hert an' lung . . . Liver . . .'

'Breast.' Aggie said, screwing up her nose once more. 'He was goin' in for a breast transplant. Well, that was it. Ah didnae want a boyfriend wi' a bigger chist than me.'

'Did ye hiv nae inklin' that he wis gay?' Alice asked.

'Ah should've guessed,' Aggie said, 'especially when Ah saw a photey of his brother's weddin'. There, posin' beautifully, was the bride an' groom and the best man and best maid.'

'So, whit made ye suspicious?' Alice asked curiously.

'*He was the best maid!*' Aggie said.

'Ah well, we live and learn,' Alice said with great wisdom.

'Did you ever get married, Alice?' Aggie asked, noticing there was no wedding ring on Wee Alice's hand.

Wee Alice shook her head. 'Naw, men didnae interest me,' she said.

'Aw, Alice, ye didnae become wan o' they thespian things, did ye?' Aggie exclaimed worriedly, adding, 'Although, mind ye, ye've got the right coupon for it.'

'Ah was too wrapped up in ma hobby and had nae time for romance,' Alice said.

'And whit wis yer hobby?' Aggie asked, drawing down her eyebrows, 'Animal impressions.'

'Ah was right intae athletics.' Alice said, 'Remember. When we were wee, Ah was always runnin'?'

'Yer nose was, right enough,' Aggie said facetiously.

Wee Alice ignored the remark.

'Ah had nae time for weans an' that,' she said, 'A' Ah wanted for tae dae was get on tae that track and race for ma country. Ah was brought tae the attention o' the Scottish Athletic selectors when Ah did the ten-hunner metres at Anniesland Park in two minutes and ten seconds.' Alice puffed out her chest.

'Ma Harry was brought tae the attention of the polis when he went tae Newton Mearns and did forty-two meters in two oors,' Aggie said.

'Forty-two metres?' Alice said. puzzled.

'A' electric!' Aggie said.

Alice let it pass. 'Anywey,' she went on, 'Ah wisnae good enough for the Olympics and there wisnae a man Ah fancied,' she shrugged, 'so Ah decided that Ah would always be a bridesmaid and never a bride.'

'So whit did ye dae?' Aggie asked.

'Well,' Alice went on, 'ma da' wanted me tae become a nun and Ah said a'right,' cos Ah wanted tae please him. But a' the wimman in ma club wur shocked when Ah announced that Ah was goin' intae a convent.'

'How was that?' Aggie asked.

'Ah was in the Orange Ludge at the time,' Alice said.

'Ye widnae have been a good nun, Alice,' Aggie said, 'Ah mean, look at ye. You're no a bit like Julie Andrews – although, lookin' at ye, Ah *can* see a connection wi' the *Sound of Music*. No "The Hills ur Alive". Mair like – yer heid is alive.'

'It's a wig,' Alice said, 'Ma hair's that lifeless that Ah started wearin' a wig two years ago. Dae ye like it?'

'Hair is a wumman's crownin' glory, Alice,' Aggie preached, 'And Ah do nut approve of wigs. Ye should be able for to manage yer own hair like every other wumman does. Get doon tae Madame Wee Nellie's doon in London Road, and she wull have ye lookin' like Farrah Fawcett instead o' a sink fawcett – a' droopin.'

'Ur ye sayin' ye don't like ma wig, then?' Alice said, hurt.

'There is wigs and there is wigs, Alice,' Aggie said, 'whit made ye choose that wan?'

'Ah saw it in a film wance an' took a fancy tae it,' Alice said.

'Whit film wis it, Alice, *Witness for the Prosecution*?' Aggie said.

'Don't scold me, Aggie,' Alice said, 'lots of wimmen wear wigs.'

'No' like Queens Council wans, they don't.' Aggie said, snidely, adding, 'Ah take it ye didnae become a nun?'

'Naw, it was too quiet for me,' Alice said. 'Ah left and Ah wanted for to get a joab wi' animals.'

'So, don't tell me,' Aggie said, 'Ye got a joab at Calderpark Zoo, right?'

'How did ye guess?' Alice said.

'By yer smell!' Aggie said, 'Ye wur stinkin' the minute ye walked in that door. At first Ah thought the vindaloo packets had burst till Ah got a right whiff.'

'Ah clean oot the elephants enclosure and Ah love ma work,' Alice said.

'Ye don't hiv tae bring yer work hame wi' ye,' Aggie said.

'Did Ah hear you mention vindaloos?' Alice asked with a grimace.

'Ye did,' Aggie said, 'And Ah'm gonny heat wan up for ye right now.'

Aggie rose and hurried towards the kitchen despite Wee Alice's protests. A quick few minutes in the microwave oven and she was back, the strong curry smell neutralizing all offending odours in the house and Wee Alice's in particular.

'Oh!' Alice cried, pushing the steaming plate away from her, 'Ah canny possibily eat *that* .' She emphasised *that*.

'*That*,' Aggie snapped, 'is good Asian cuisine. It came from the bowels of India and ye can tell that by the smell. It reminds you of elephants an' that and you should be well acquainted wi' the elephant connection. So get it doon ye and enjoy yersel"

'Ah canny,' Alice said, 'Ah'm a vegan.'

'Yer sexual status has nuthin' tae dae wi it. Jist eat.'

Nancy who had been quietly following her mother's dialogue with her maid of honour finally broke her silence.

'She means she disnae eat meat, Mammy,' she said.

'Ah know that, Ah know that,' Aggie said repeating herself and flushed with embarrassment. 'They'll no' even eat wulks. No anybody that wullnae eat wulks must hiv somethin' wrang wi' them. Wulks were put on this earth, albeit under the watter, for to be picked up and biled. They ur there for oor pleasure. Ah mean they hiv nae brains. They jist lie there – waitin' or maybe shakin' wi' fear a wee bit right enough, but they know the inevitable.'

'Ah can not eat any livin' thing that's deid,' Alice said.

'Nae wonder ye're so skinny,' Aggie said.

'You're very lucky, Aggie, tae hiv such a carin' daughter and tae hiv had a good man,' Alice said, changing the subject.

'Ah realise that, Alice,' Aggie said with a deep sigh. 'Ye missed oot, hen,' she added. 'Ah know ye wur contemplatin' goin' intae a life of contemplation but when ye came oot ye should've tried for to find a handsome young man fur yersel'. Or, wi' a coupon like yours, an ugly auld man would have sufficed.'

Alice drew Aggie a scathing look.

Aggie removed the vindaloo and returned it to the kitchen.

'You'll be Aggie's daughter, then, eh?' Alice said, turning to Nancy.

'Aye, Ah'm Nancy,' Nancy said.

'Wi' the laughin' face, eh?' Alice said, with a laugh.

'Only when she's got her teeth in,' Aggie said, coming in at the tail end of the conversation.

They all laughed. Deep down, Aggie was delighted to have Alice with them. Okay, she didn't eat meat and that meant one left over vindaloo. Her presence was the main thing. She watched Alice laughing and wondered what she had to laugh about. Her wee pal had never enjoyed the warmth of a family. No loving husband to keep her warm on cold, winter nights. No son or daughter there with all the fighting and arguments that go into the family boiling pot. Only to be spooned out when all is forgiven and the pot is cooled down. She was here to join in Aggie's celebrations and that was what mattered. Wee Alice was a true friend.

It was as though wee Alice was reading Aggie's thoughts. Her eyes took on a faraway look and a smile crossed her lips. 'Ye know,' she said, 'Ah nearly fell in love wance.'

'Ye don't say, Alice,' Aggie said, raising her eyebrows.

'It was in a lounge bar,' Alice went on. 'Ah felt like a wee sherry for ma chist and sat on a stool at the bar.'

'That's disgustin',' Aggie said, interrupting. 'It's probably been a dug that did it. Some people have nae sense o' decency. Imagine allowin' yer wee dug tae sit on a seat that somebody was gonny sit on wi' their nice, clean claeths.'

Aggie screwed up her nose and said. 'Yeuch!'

'Naw, ye don't understaun', Aggie,' Alice said. 'Ah was sittin' sippin' ma drink when Ah noticed this big handsome fella sittin' on a stool at the other end o' the bar lookin' at me.'

'Probably couldnae believe his eyes,' Aggie said.

'That's the operative word *eyes*. Ah was a' a-flutter when he rolled his big brown eyes at me.' Alice clasped her chest.

'So, whit did ye dae, pick them up n' roll them back?' Aggie said with a cheeky grin.

'But Ah'm afraid Ah was in for a disappointment. It wisnae me he was lookin' at.' Alice gave a long sigh. 'It was the barman.'

'Wis he gay?' Aggie asked, seeing the disappointment in Wee Alice's eyes.

'He looked happy enough,' Alice said.

'Naw, Ah meant was he queer?'

'Aye, come tae think of it,' Alice said. 'Ah should've guessed, so Ah should've when Ah noticed the very smart uniform he was wearin' especially in a dump like that.'

'Whit uniform was he wearin' that made ye think that there was somethin' queer aboot him?' Aggie asked.

'Gestapo!'

'Aye, well, that should've telt ye somethin' right enough. Maybe ye jist thought it was a Gestapo uniform. Ah mean he could've jist been a traffic warden or somethin' there's no' much difference. Did his cap have a skull on it?' Aggie was intrigued.

'Aye, it did, Aggie,' Alice said, placing her forefinger on her cheek and thinking back. 'Whit dae *you* know aboot skulls?'

'Harry used tae be oot o' his every Saturday night,' Aggie said.

'Ah was really dumped, so Ah was,' Alice said.

'Aye, there's no' many good-lookin' young men goin' aboot even today,' Aggie said. 'Although you should've been gled o' an auld ugly man.' Aggie followed this up by pecking Alice's cheek.

'Ah never did get a man tae love me,' Alice said sadly. 'Whit aboot you, Nancy,' she added turning to Aggie's daughter who had been listening intently to the conversation.

Aggie put a protective arm around Nancy's shoulders.

'Nancy isnae like that, Alice, she said. She is nut wan o' them les beans, or whitever ye call them She is a *man*'s wumman. Her only claim tae bein' gay is that she laughs a lot.'

'Naw, Ah didnae mean that,' Alice protested. 'Ah meant has *she* got a man in her life . . . a boyfriend?'

'She is winchin' a midget right noo and is savin' up, although she is nut tellin' me whit she is savin' up for,' Aggie said, drawing Nancy a look.

'Ah'm saving up for when he gets oot,' Nancy said.

'Aw, is the wee sowel in hospital?' Alice said with a sad expression.

'Naw, he's in Barlinnie,' Nancy said. 'Glasgow's famous jail.'

'Oh my!' Alice said.

'He's in for a stretch,' Aggie volunteered.

'Well Ah wish ye well, hen,' Alice said to Nancy. 'Ye've got a man, wee or no', and that's mair than Ah've got.'

'Never mind, Alice,' Aggie said, 'somewhere in this world is a wee, auld ugly man looking for a wee auld ugly wumman like you.'

'That's the nicest thing anybody has ever said tae me,' Alice said, dabbing her eye.

'Och, whit are freen's for, Alice?' Aggie said. 'Noo, you jist sit there and Ah'll get ye somethin' nice tae eat – hauf-a-pun' of turnip or somethin?'

Alice shook her head. 'Naw, naw, Aggie,' she said, 'don't go tae any bother. Ah've got tae run. Ah've got an appointment wi' ma ciropractor.'

'Ye . . . ye mean ye're no' steyin for ma celebrations?' Aggie was dumped.

'He's a very busy man, ma chiropractor,' Alice said, 'An Ah don't want tae miss ma appointment.'

'Ye don't want ma vindaloos and noo ye don't want ma turnip?' Aggie said sadly.

'It's no' that, Aggie,' Alice said with a hint of contrition.

'Yer chiropractor! Aggie shook her head. ' Could ye no' gie up yer singin' lessons for *wan* night?'

'Ah'm sorry, Aggie,' Alice said. 'But Ah'll need tae go. Ah hope ye have a wonderful night – you and yer guests.'

'Whit guests? Me, Nancy an' the mice?' Aggie murmured, adding mournfully, 'Ah should've got in a pun o' cheese.'

Alice got up and turning to Nancy, said, 'Wull ye see me doon tae the bus, hen? That stalker might be aboot.'

'Aye, right,' Nancy said, 'come on, Ah'll no' be long, Mammy.'

Wee Alice pecked Aggie's cheek. 'Happy anniversary, Aggie,' she said, dabbed her eyes and hurried out followed by Nancy.

Aggie went to the door and called out. 'Be careful noo. Ah read there's a psychopath goin' aboot here attackin' young lassies. Jist watch yersels. Cheerio Alice.'

Aggie closed the door and taking her wedding photograph from the sideboard, placed it on the table. She sat gazing at it.

'Well, Harry,' she said sadly. 'Two down and two dozen vindaloos tae go. It would seem that naebody wants tae celebrate oor golden weddin' wi' me. Ach, well, it's time like these when ye know who yer feens are, int it?'

She kissed the picture and replaced it in its place of honour and flopped back on the the chair. She *did* worry about Nancy and Wee Alice's safety. There *had* been a spate of violent attacks recently. But, then again, Aggie worried about lots of things.

She wondered just whereabouts in the body Alice's chiro was?

CHAPTER TWO

NANCY STILL HAD NOT RETURNED FROM SEEING WEE ALICE TO the bus stop. Aggie pulled back the curtain and let her eyes sweep the quiet street. Not a sign of life! She returned to her easy chair. She did not hear the slight squealing of car brakes outside her house or the slamming of a car door. A loud rapping at her door made her jump.

She hurried to the door, stopping, momentarily, to buff up her hair at the wall mirror.

'Aggie!' The large woman in the silver fox fur cried in delight and enveloped her in a pair of strong arms. The whiff of expensive perfume filled Aggie's nostrils. The large lady swept on into the room and planted herself in the easy chair, leaning back and spreading her legs out.

'And, how's it goin', me auld china?' she bellowed.

Aggie stared at the woman. Who was she? Aggie could not place her and the big woman shook her head.

'Aggie, ye don't recognise me, dae ye?'

'Jist gie me a minute,' Aggie said, 'Ah jist canny place ye.'

'It's *me* . . . yer auld pal!'

'Gie me a hint,' Aggie said.

The big woman jumped up and, with her arms swaying in the air, began to sing in true 'Tevye' fashion from *Fiddler on the Roof.* 'If I were a rich man – da, da, da, da da, da da . . .'

'Ah'm thinkin'. Ah'm thinkin',' Aggie said,

'Ach, whit kinda hint dae ye want?' the lady said.

'Gie me another hint,' Aggie said.

The big lady cleared her throat and burst into song – 'People, people who need people', 'There,' she said.

'Ye're . . . ye're . . . ye're no' *Barbra Streisand*, are ye?' Aggie stammered.

'Oh, aye,' the lady scoffed, 'Ye think Barbra Streisand turns tae Metro Goldwyn Mayer's boss and said, 'Sorry Ah canny dae that film ye want tae pey me ten million dollars for, Ah'm flyin' ower tae Brigton for tae be a guest at ma auld pal Aggie's golden weddin' anniversary.'

'So, ye're no' Barbra Streisand – and ye're no' Topol and you are definitely no' Betty Grable. Ah'm sorry, hen, ye've past me,' Aggie said. 'Try again!'

'It's *me*,' the woman said at last, throwing up her arms . . . '*Me* – Esther – Esther Goldberg. How could you forget, Aggie?'

'Aye, how could Ah forget you, Esther ma auld pal. Remember when we were wee lassies and we used tae get stoapped by ruffians who demanded "Ur you a Billy or a Dan?" and Ah used for to say, "a Billy", and you used tae say, "a Moses".'

They both laughed and Aggie hugged Esther tightly, saying, 'Ye've chinged, Esther.'

'Geez, it's been fifty years, Aggie,' Esther said.

'Ye're name wisnae Goldberg then, so it wisnae,' Aggie said, 'Did ye chinge it 'cos ye looked a bit like Whoopi?'

'Don't be daft. Whoopi Goldberg is a black wumman,' Esther said, smiling and digging Aggie in the ribs.

'Ah've been havin' trouble wi' ma eyes,' Aggie said.

'Goldberg is ma merried name,' Esther said.

'Aye Ah remember you had an Irish name if Ah am correct it was . . . it was Esther O'Jacobs or somethin' . . . that right?'

Esther laughed loudly. 'Aye, that's right,' she said.

'Yer da' was a jeweller?'

'He worked for a jeweller,' Esther said, 'Ah mean we *did* live in a single-end, Aggie. Ye don't get WH Samuels livin' up a close. Naw, he *worked* for a jeweller.'

'Ah don't care if yer name's Tiffany. Ye're here noo and that's a' that metters.'

Aggie was truly delighted. Harry would be over the moon if he could reach that height from where he was.

'Oh, here,' Aggie exclaimed, 'Ah never did pey ye for that paste tiara ye made for me for ma weddin' dress, remember?'

'Why dae think Ah'm here,' Esther laughed and with Aggie joining in.

'Sorry, but Ah jist don't have the money right noo for tae settle things wi' ye,' Aggie said.

'That's a'right,' Esther said. 'Ah take credit cerds.'

Esther produced a credit card machine and laid it on her lap.

'Whit have ye got – Visa or Mastercard?'

'Visa,' Aggie said handing over her card.

Esther swiped the card through the machine and handed it back.

'Ah'm no' chargin' ye interest,' she said.

'Thank God for that,' Aggie said.

Aggie poured out two drinks.

'Happy anniversary, hen,' Esther said, knocking her drink back in one go.

'Whit aboot yersel'?' Aggie said, smacking her lips. 'Did ye ever get married?'

'Ah did,' Esther said, 'To a lovely wee man, God Rest his soul.' She clasped her hands to her breast and looked skywards.

'Aw, whit a shame!' Aggie said. 'We're baith in the same boat. Did he leave you well embowled?'

'Aye, well, ma Jacob was a hard worker. He had his ain wee jewellery business. And Ah kept it oan efter he went on tae higher things. Business isnae too bad and Ah'm kept goin'. In fact Ah just got an order in the other day for a tiara, no' unlike your wan, only wi' real diamonds an' that and wi' the promise of a jewel-studded crown to follow.'

'That's good!' Aggie said, 'Who ordered that?'

'Some wumman called Camila Parker something,' Esther said.

'Bowles,' Aggie volunteered.

'Aye, that's whit Ah say,' Esther said. And, holding out her glass for a re-fill, went on, 'Aye, it's been a long time, hen, eh? Fifty years, who would believe it.'

'Aye,' Aggie said, 'it was fifty glorious years. And noo it's ma golden anniversary,' she said, happily.

'Whit aboot Harry?' Esther said.

'Aye, it's his as well,' Aggie said.

'Where is Harry?' Esther asked.

'If Ah know ma Harry he is sittin' somewhere right noo wi' a harp in his hauns,' Aggie said.

'Sittin' happily playin' it?' Esther said.

'Drinkin' it,' Aggie retorted, adding softly, 'Esther, ma Harry passed away five years ago.'

'Aw, Ah didnae know, Aggie,' Esther said. 'Whit happened? Did he have a heart attack? Cos Ah always remember your Harry was a keen keep fit wee man.' Thinking back she said, 'Remember he used tae go cycle racin'? And mind that time he came in first in that cycle race tae Helensburgh? First oot o' fifty-two racin' cyclists, no' bad goin', eh?'

Aggie nodded, 'Right enough,' she said, 'especially when he didnae hiv a bike.'

Esther commiserated. 'Ma poor Jacob is gone noo, tae,' she said. 'He got his wish, but. Ah got him buried in the Holy Land.'

Aggie's brows shot up. 'Ah didnae know the Ibrox directors allowed that,' she said.

'Naw, naw, in Jerusalem,' Esther said, 'on the Mount of Olives, where everybody wants to get buried.'

'Ah don't,' Aggie said. 'Ah don't like olives, except in Martinis maybe. Besides, Ah want for to be crematised.'

Aggie poured another drink. 'You – er never made it tae yer Golden, then. Eh?'

'Oh, aye,' Esther said, 'Ah made it jist a few weeks ago. Ah knew Jacob would've wanted it that wey, so he would've.'

'Yer Golden Weddin' Anniversary, eh?' Aggie was impressed.

'Aye, but Ah called it ma Goldberg Weddin' Anniversary, efter Jacob, y'know.'

'Ah know whit ye mean,' Aggie said, 'Good joab Jacob's name wisnae Jacob Crap.'

They both laughed.

'Hiv ye any weans?' Aggie asked.

Esther nodded. 'Oh, aye. Jacob was a real hurricane in bed, so he was,' Esther said.

'So was ma Harry,' Aggie said, 'full o' wind.'

'Ah've got a boy – Rueben,' Esther said.

' That' a nice Welsh name,' Aggie said.

'He's chingin' it for business reasons,' Esther said, not sound-ing too pleased.

'Oh! Whit's he chingin' it tae?' Aggie asked.

'Hymie,' Esther said.

'Aw, that's a nice name, tae,' Aggie said, 'French!'

'Ye'd think he would go through life wi' the name his maw had gied him.' Esther was hurt.

'Aye, but some weans jist don't suit the names they were gied,' Aggie said. 'Ah mean, Ah know that some weans these day are called efter television and fitba' stars an' that. But it's later on in life that it just disnae suit them. Ah mean look at young Molly McTavish doon the road. She's jist had a wean and bein' in fashion, has called him Romeo. Ah mean, Ah ask ye. Can ye imagine her hingin' oot the windae an' bawlin' "Hey Romeo McTavish, you come in for yer dinner this minute".'

'Jacob was that proud o' him,' Esther said, 'he would be real hurt if he knew that he had chinged his name.'

'Aye, right enough, A can understaun' that,' Aggie said. 'Jacob, bein' a good Jewish faither would want his son to keep the name he was Christened wi.'

Esther let that go. 'Jacob lavished everythin'on him. Rueben's barmitzvah was the talk o' the steamie.'

'How was that?' Aggie asked.

'It was held in the steamie,' Esther said.

'Whit's a barmitzvah?' Aggie asked.

'That's when Rueben became a man,' Esther said.

'How? Whit was he before it – a wumman?' Aggie asked, puzzled.

'Don't be daft,' Esther said. 'It's when a young Jewish boy changes from being a boy and becomes a man. He becomes of age, know whit Ah mean?'

'We don't have anythin' like that in oor faith,' Aggie said. 'We jist know when oor wee boys become men is when they stoap buyin' the *Beano* and start buyin' *Playboy.*'

Esther laughed. 'Aye, he's ma boy,' she said, 'he's a big son and Ah'm proud o' him. He was born in a trunk in a West End theatre and Jacob and me were sure that was an omen, that his destiny was showbusiness and he would become a big star.'

'And did he?' Aggie asked,

'Naw, he's in charge o' the left luggage office in Central station,' Esther said.

'Well, it was an omen, really, wint it?' Aggie said, 'Born in a trunk an' a' that.'

'Aye,' Esther said, 'Ah suppose so. Takin' that premise he

might've turned oot tae be a hard case.'

Their eyes met and they burst out laughing.

'Whit were you daein' in a trunk, anyway?' Aggie said.

'Jacob and me were on holiday in the Holy Land at the time and had gone tae the theatre for to see a play a freen' o' mine was in and it was when we were in her dressin room that Rueben decided to make his entry,' Esther smiled as she recalled.

'Was Rueben in the play as well, then?' Aggie asked.

'Don't be daft,' Esther said.

'Ye said he made his entrance,' Aggie said.

'He decided to come into the world,' Esther said. 'Ah was jist staunin' there when suddenly Ah went *Oh!* and fell intae the trunk and Rueben arrived screamin' in the middle of act two.'

'A crap play, was it?' Aggie said. 'Him screamin' an' that.'

'Naw, naw, the play was nothin' to do wi' his screamin',' Esther said, 'he was too wee to understand it – it was wan o' Shakespeare's greatest comedy's.'

'Whit wis it – the *Steamie*?' Aggie asked.

'Naw, Ah think it was *Lions Versus the Christians*,' Esther said.

'Ach, Ah hate they zoo plays,' Aggie said. 'So, does that mean that your boy, being born in the Holy Land, is a foreigner?'

'Naw, naw, he's British,' Esther said. 'He's been nationalised.'

'But surely wee Jewish boys get that done anyway,' Aggie said, 'no matter where they're born? The rabbit does it, dint he?'

'It's a different word, Aggie,' Esther said. 'Anywey, as Ah was sayin', he had a lovely barmitzvah in the steamie. Ma Jacob was a shrewd man. No matter how much they ate, they could be as sick as they liked and a' we had tae dae was pop their claeths straight intae the washin'-tub.'

'And that was yer boy a man noo, eh?' Aggie was full of admiration.

'Aye, that was him a man,' Esther said proudly.

'Aye, Ah suppose it's good for to be recognised as a man – although oor neighbour in the the auld buildin' hated it.'

'Whit was yer neighbour's name?' Esther asked.

'Annie Sweeney,' Aggie said. 'She was the only wumman in the street that went roon the back courts singin'. As soon as she went roon the back and started, up went hunners o' windaes. Folk jist couldnae believe that wonderful voice. A loat o'people thought it was that marvellous black singer . . .' Aggie hesitated.

'Ella Fitzgerald?' Esther volunteered.

'Paul Robeson,' Aggie said.

Esther smiled

'Still. Ah'm gled for your wee Rue . . . er . . . Hymie,' Aggie said, 'Ma Harry would've loved for to have been Jewish and be involved in that barmvitzvah ceremony, so he would've. Anythin' wi' the word *Bar* in it, he was all for it.'

'Dae ye really think your Harry would've liked to have been of oor faith?' Esther asked, surprised.

Aggie screwed up her nose. 'Oh, aye, he loved curries, but Ah don't really suppose he would've needed for to go through that barmitzvah thing cos Harry was a boy a' his life. That would never have chinged him.'

'That was just a symbol,' Esther said.

'Oh, Harry liked them,' Aggie said, 'He used tae play them in the Orange Baun.'

While Aggie was enjoying the chat with her old friend, she was worried because Nancy had not returned from her escort duty with Wee Alice. Also, nobody else had shown up. She would wander over to the window, pull the curtain back and stare into the empty street, sigh and return to the conversation.

Esther looked well. She looked as though she had just stepped out of a fashion catalogue. Life had been good to her and her wealth had not gone to her head. Still, she had her worries, too. This son of hers sounded as though he was "not the full shullin". If he was going to change his name for business reasons, Aggie thought, why change it from Rueben to Hymie? That was daft and served no purpose, she thought. There *are* times when a change of name can be an advantage. Actor Arnold Schwarzenegger could never have got away with a tag like that in the old days of cinema when even William Beadle had to change his name to William Holden. Big Arnie, Aggie thought should've changed his name to, say, Fred Schwarzenegger. But Rueben to Hymie, what did it tell you!

Esther was still talking.

'I was surprised to see by his photo that Harry was completely bald. I always remember him with a good head of hair.'

'There was naebody mair surprised than Harry when every hair in his heid a' started for tae fight wi' wan another.'

Esther drew her brows together.

'His hairs a' started tae fight wi' one another? Whit dae ye mean?' she asked, puzzled.

'They a' fell oot,' Aggie said with a chuckle.

'Aw, Ah see,' Esther cried and joined in the laughing.

'Ye're right, tae,' Aggie aid, 'Harry *did* have a good heid o' hair – red and wirey, it was. Ah blame his faither for takin' the strength oot o' it. When Harry was wee his hair was that wirey that his faither used for to grab his heid and rub it up an' doon the wa' for to strip the wall paper.'

'Did his maw no' say anythin'?' Esther asked.

'She was too busy haudin' his legs,' Aggie said.

'That is cruelty, so it is,' Esther said.

'It got worse,' Aggie went on. 'When his heid wisnae daein' the trick, they made him swally petrol, make him open his mooth wide, haud him facin' the wa' and put a match up tae his mooth.'

'A match?' Esther said.

'A Swan Vesta,' Aggie said. 'A jet o' flame came oot and did the joab. The paper jist peeled away.'

'How horrible!' Esther said with a grimace.

'It was tae haunt him the rest of his life,' Aggie said. 'He was very passionate. Oan oor first kiss up the close he opened his gub and took ma eyebrows clean aff. Ah could see then why the other lassies called him *Hot Lips*. Ye could tell every other lassie he had dated. Every wan o' them was baldy and had nae eyebrows.'

'But ye still loved him. Eh?' Esther said.

'Oh, aye. He was great for getting' the fire started in the moarnins.'

'Poor Harry!' Esther said. 'He had terrible parents.'

'Ye're right there,' Aggie said. 'His faither used tae come intae the hoos every Setturday night stotious drunk and beat Harry's maw.'

'Beat his maw?' Esther tutted.

'Only by aboot ten minutes right enough,' Aggie said.

'Aye, well, Ah've got a lot for to be thankful for,' Esther said.

'Ma faither was the kindest man in the world, so he was. As a young man he had tae flee his home in Europe tae avoid persecution. He arrived in this country penniless. He had hidden amongst fourteen hundred stinkin', smelly pigs on board a cattle boat and him a good Jewish boy tae.'

'God bless 'im,' Aggie said.

'It took six months before anybody would gie him a joab,' Esther said, bitterly.

'Because he was a Jew?' Aggie said.

'Because he stank,' Esther said. 'But he soon got absorbed intae the Jewish community in Glesca. The rabbi felt sorry for him and thought he should have a wife cos he looked so lonely. He used for to throw hints at him and then wan Saturday as ma faither was leavin' the synagogue, the rabbi stoapped him and haunded him a copy of the *Jewish Gazette* and stapled on Page three was copy of the widow Cominsky's bank balance.'

'Ah've heard o' that widow Cominsky,' Aggie said. 'She had a big heart.'

'She had a big everything,' Esther said. 'But especially a bank balance. But ma faither wisnae interested. He still thought aboot ma mother but took comfort knowing that she would be warm in the coming winter.'

'How was that?' Aggie asked.

'She was workin' in a Siberian coal mine,' Esther said.

'So, ye had nae maw in yer life, Esther?' Aggie said sadly.

'Oh, aye. Ma faither met another wumman, here, in Glesca. He was walkin' past a café in Sauchiehall Street wan day when he heard screamin' comin' frae the inside. Bein' the gentleman he was, he dashed inside and saw this lovely wumman sittin' on a stool.'

'These dugs are everywhere,' Aggie said screwing up her nose, 'but carry on, Esther, sorry Ah interrupted ye.'

''Sittin' on a stool takin' her nail polish aff.'

'Why the screams?' Aggie asked.

'She was usin' a blow lamp,' Esther said.

'And yer da' fell in love right away, eh? How romantic,' Aggie fluttered her eyelashes and sighed.

'Naw, no' right away,' Esther said. 'It wisnae till later when he suddenly began tae appreciate her intellect that he took her in his erms and swore undyin' love for her.'

'Whit made him chinge his mind?' Aggie asked,

'It was wan day – a bright sunny, summer's day it was – he went to visit her for to see how the burns on her haun' was healing and found her sittin' roon' the back near the midden, readin' a big, heavy very interestin' book. He saw how hard it was for her to turn the pages, her wi' her bandaged haun' and oaffered tae turn them for her. As he turned the pages for to see whit she was readin' his eyes widened and he immediately appreciated her and proposed there and then right on the spot.'

'That must've been some book,' Aggie said, 'Whit was it – *War and Peace – Gone with the Wind*?'

''Her bank book,' Esther said.

'Aye, well, money disnae always bring ye happiness,' Aggie said. 'Ah got a' excited as Ah watched the telly, checkin' ma lottery numbers. Ah had six numbers.'

'Don't tell me ye won the lettery?' Esther said.

'Naw, they were a' wrang,' Aggie said.

'It's better for to earn yer money,' Esther said. 'Ye get mair satisfaction oot o' it. When ma faither arrived here he had jist wan thing tae his name – a needle and a bobbin of black thread, that wis a'.'

'That's two things,' Aggie said.

Esther ignored the remark.

'Within days he had two needles and a bobbin of *white* thread and there was nae stoappin' him from then on. Within ninety-seven years he had the tailorin' trade in Glesca a' sewn up.'

'Aw, that's wonderful,' Maggie said. 'Jist think – if he'd got a bobbin of coloured thread he might've had it a' sewed up in aboot eighty-two years.'

'Whit aboot *your* faither?' Esther asked.

'Naw, he couldnae sew,' Aggie said. 'He arrived in Glesca wi' jist a toothbrush an' nuthin' else.'

'Sad!' Esther said.

'He had nae money but a nice smile,' Aggie said. 'Oh, here,' she suddenly said. 'How aboot a wee cup of tea?' Aggie held a tea bag over the teapot. 'Or would ye like somethin' a bit stronger?' she added.

'Stronger,' Esther said without hesitation.

And so Aggie popped in *two* teabags.

'Ah wonder whit's keepin' Nancy?' she said with a worried expression.

Aggie poured the tea and they clinked teacups.

'Cheers,' Aggie said.

'Mahzaltov!' Esther said.

'That's a word ma Harry used for to use,' Aggie said.

'Mahzaltov?' Esther was surprised. 'Don't tell me Harry was really Jewish,' she said.

'Naw, but he *wis* a great fan o' Charleton Heston,' Aggie said.

'But Charleton Heston isnae Jewish,' Esther said.

'So whit was he daein' goin' up that mountain black heided and staggerin doon. Humpin' two big lumps o' stane, and lookin' like Santy Claus?'

'That was jist a part he was playin' in *The Ten Commandments*,' Esther said. 'He is an actor. Actors are no' really the people they portray on the screen, Aggie. They're jist . . . er . . . well . . . er . . . actin'.'

'Ah know that,' Aggie said. 'But ye dae get cerried away, don't ye?'

Esther laughed. 'Ye're an awful wumman, Aggie,' she said.

'Er whit exactly does mahzaltov mean,' Aggie asked.

'Well, Ah suppose it means "Good Luck" an' that,' Esther said.

'Aw, that's nice,' Aggie said. 'It's got a nice ring tae it. A loat nicer than whit we say, "Aw rabest' an that". Y'know, ma Nancy was nearly impregnated intae the Jewish faith wance.'

'Oh, how was that?'

'Well, wan day ma Nancy was walkin' alang the street when she tripped and fell and hurt her leg. Well a young Jewish doctor was passin' at the time and stoapped tae help her.'

'How did she know he was Jewish?' Esther asked.

'He had gold fillin's in his teeth – twenty four carat,' Aggie said.

'How did she know that?'

'He took them oot and showed her them,' Aggie said.

'Did he charge her for his services?'

'He did not,' Aggie said.

'He wisnae Jewish,' Esther said.

'Aye, he was,' Aggie said, 'and they started a relationship.'

The light-hearted chat was fine but Aggie was still worried. No Dolly, no Alice no Nancy, even. Thank heaven for Esther. Harry had always liked Esther and Jacob. She looked up at the clock. Time was going on. Lucky, she thought, the vidaloos take only minutes in the micro-wave.

'Ye've nae idea how much Ah appreciate ye comin', Esther,' she said.

'Ah widnae have missed yer celebrations for the world,' Esther said.

'You've never let me down – ever,' Aggie said.

Esther bowed her head, slightly embarrassed.

'Mind the time when Nancy was a wean and Ah couldnae afford buyin' her a school uniform for John Street School? Ah came tae you and explained ma plight.'

'Aye, Ah remember, Aggie,' Esther said. 'A' the other weans looked bright as buttons on that first day at school.'

'Ah was embarrassed,' Aggie said. 'Especially when the other weans started callin' Nancy *Wurzel*. Weans can be cruel! But it was *you* Esther, that came to the rescue and solved the problem.'

'Ah'm tryin' tae remember whit Ah did, Aggie,' Esther said. 'Did Ah get ye a full school uniform hauf price or somethin'?'

'Naw, ye got Nancy expelled. That outfit ye gave us jist didnae fit in wi' that good school, named efter John Knox,' Aggie said.

'Well, that's understandable,' Esther said, 'Efter all Ah am nut cognizant wi' your religious institutions.'

'Ah remember it fine,' Aggie said, 'the headmistress turned blue in the face when Nancy walked in that day. A' dressed up like a little sister of the Poor.'

'Aye, well, it was a genuine mistake,' Esther said. 'So, she got expelled, did she?'

'Oh. Aye, and that saved me hivin' tae scrape thegither the money for a school uniform. It a' turned oot well. Comin' hame she collected three pounds frae devout Catholics she met in the street.'

'So, whit's happened tae yer other guests, Aggie? Should they no' be here by this time?' Esther said.

'Ah was hopin'ma brother Sammy would've been here by this time,' Aggie said. 'He finds it hard tae get away right enough. He's involved wi' wan o' the Queen's institutions. Mind ye, Sammy was always unpredictable. He was the black sheep o' the family. He was a weakly wean when he was born and the doactor was never away frae oor hoose. Ma maw always said his illness was an omen that he was gonny turn oot the black sheep.'

'Whit did the doactor say was up wi' him?' Esther asked.

'Foot and Mouth,' Aggie said.

'Ach, away wi' ye,' Esther said giving Aggie a gentle push.

'Oh, ye've nae idea how really pleased I am tae see ye, Esther,' Aggie said. 'If naebody else turns up at least you and me will celebrate. Ah'll no' be alone.'

Esther smiled. 'Ah'm gled for tae be here, hen,' she said.

Esther did not appreciate how much Aggie welcomed her prescence. This was the night she had planned for so long. She knew Harry would be more pleased to know that she had kept her promise. They had a happy life and Aggie bent over backwards to keep him happy. Harry even began to wear Indian clothes, bringing him memories of his time with the army and Aggie hadn't complained. He even attached a bead to his nose with super glue. For Harry had insisted that everything should be authentic and had prised it off, boring a hole in his nostril with a hand-cranked drill. But she didn't mind. She knew Harry liked a good bead in him.

Aggie, once again, went to the window and peered down into the quiet street. Still no sign of Nancy, Alice or even the stalker. 'Ah wonder whit's keepin' Nancy?' she said worriedly.

'Ach. Don't worry.' Esther said. 'She's probably still waitin' for a bus. Ye know whit buses are like? They're like bananas. They come in bunches.'

A smile crossed Aggie's face but it was a false smile.

A sudden rapping at the door made her jump. Startled, but with hopes rising, she hurried to answer. She would give Nancy a piece of her mind for taking so long and leaving her without fingernails.

Aggie opend the door wide. He stood there, arms outstretched. The gold tooth in his upper plate flashed as the hall light caught it and the thin, Ronald Coleman moustache twitched with his broad smile.

'Aggie,' he cried, sweeping her into his arms. 'Ye look a million dollars, hen, so ye dae – no' a day aulder.' He said, kissing her on the cheek. 'Ah jist couldnae let yer golden weddin' go by without drappin' in. Here, this is for you.' The wee man handed Aggie a canvas bag from which she produced a large, heavy golden chain.

'Gold, for yer golden day,' he said, kissing her again.

Aggie held the chain out at arms lengeth and smiled broadly.

'Aw, int that lovely!' she said. 'Ye're a wee gem, Sammy, so ye ur rememberin' ma golden weddin'.'

Turning to Esther, who was looking puzzled at the new arrival Aggie cried oot, 'This is ma brother, Sammy,' she said, steering him into the room, 'and this is ma good freen' Esther Goldberg.'

Sammy took Esther's hand in his and kissed it gently.

'Ah am pleased for to meet you,' he said, 'Ah was nut cognizant of the fact that Aggie had any Welsh freens.'

Esther pulled her hand away. 'Ah am nut Welsh,' she said, 'Ah'm frae Newton Mearns.'

This affluent area of Glasgow was known to Sammy because of his many visits to houses there – usually uninvited.

'It's a beautiful chain, Sammy,' Aggie extolled, 'it wull look lovely in the lavvy, so it wull – it must've cost ye a bomb, Sammy, eh?'

Sammy gave a slight cough. 'The gentleman from whom Ah acquired it mentioned nothin' aboot it's value,' he said.

'Well, he must've been flush for to hiv a lavvy chain like that,' Aggie said.

'Ye hivnae chinged a bit, Aggie,' Sammy said, 'same teeth, same hair, same nose like the horn at John Brown's shipyerd.'

Sammy's insulting remarks were lost on Aggie, who was just delighted that another guest had turned up for the celebrations.

'Er . . . did ye ever get married, Sammy?' she asked.

Sammy puckered his lip. 'Noo, there lies a tale,' he said. 'Ah married ma optician's daugher, a man, knowin' the state of ma eyes, conned me. It was months before Ah realised that she had a face like a gumsy hoarse and it was her faither tae blame. No' only for her face but for how Ah saw her – beautiful.'

'How was that, then?' Aggie asked drawing down her brows.

'He had painted a picture of Rita Hayworth on the lenses o ma new specs. Ah should've known all along, so Ah should've,' Sammy sounded bitter.

Esther hid a smile.

'How did ye find oot?' Aggie asked.

'Wan day Ah drapped ma specs and they broke. Ah bent doon and picked them up and put them oan. And when Ah stood up there she was staunin' there smiln' – a dead ringer for Red Rum. Wi' a bit o' trainin' Ah could've entered her for the Grand National. Ah swore there an' then that Ah would never get married again and that Ah'd chinge ma optician.'

Esther could not contain herself. 'Ye're nae oil paintin' yersel,' she said.

'Huh! Listen tae auld Goldfinger, there,' Sammy growled.

'He's got ye there, Esther,' Aggie said. 'There was naebody in oor family mair well oiled than oor Sammy, so there wisnae.'

Both women burst out laughing.

'Aye, well whit aboot your Harry, Aggie? Did he ever make anythin' o' himsel'? Sammy said. 'He was always an ambitious wee man who liked his dram.'

'He gave up drinkin' the day he died,' Aggie said.

'How did he die?' Sammy asked.

'Ah'm no' tellin' ye,' Aggie said.

'Did he still have that "get-up'an' go" attitude?' Sammy asked.

'Aye, well, the phrasin' was chinged a bit,' Aggie said. 'Ah used tae go intae the bedroom in the moarnin' and gie him a shake and encourage him sayin' "C'mon, get up an' go".' Aggie shook her head. 'But that was eventually chinged tae just, "C'mon get up".'

Esther stood up and with a puzzled expression said, 'Here, let me see that chain.'

Aggie handed her the heavy chain and Esther examined it closely and with interest.

'Lovely, intit?' Aggie said proudly. 'They wee bits of coloured gless jist add tae it, no' think so, Esther?'

Esther produced a jeweller's eye-glass and examined it more closely. Then, looking up in triumph, declared, 'These are nut wee bits of gless, Aggie. These are gem stones.'

'Gem stones?' Aggie cried, 'Ah should've known. There's nothin' hammy aboot oor Sammy. He does nothing by haufs -- maybe a few haufs in him, right enough. But Gem stones, eh?' She clicked her tongue.

'Hammy is nut a word you should use in front of Missus Goldfish, here,' Sammy scolded.

Esther shrugged. 'It disnae bother me,' she said, 'jist like people who tell porky pies.' She drew Sammy a look.

'How come you know so much aboot gems anyway?' Sammy said.

''Cos she's in the same business as you,' Aggie said.

'Ye mean ye're a thief?' Sammy said raising his brows.

'Naw, she's in the jewellery business,' Aggie said. 'She makes it and you steal it. Youse work wi' the same commodity.'

Sammy was suddenly very impressed with this friend of his sister's. 'Well, now, imagine that, eh?' he smiled. 'You ur in the jewellery business, how about that, then, eh?'

His eyes rolled like the spinners on a Las Vegas casino machine and his adrenalin raced like a man who was about to hit the jackpot. Esther had seen these signs before. Sammy's face had a royal flush in diamonds. She set her jaw and waited for the patter.

'So, you're in the jewellery business, eh?' Sammy repeated himself. 'There's ony wan thing Ah can say tae that,' he added, once more kissing Esther's hand.

'An' whit's that?' Esther asked. Eyes narrowing.

'Wull ye mairry me?' Sammy said, his gold tooth flashing.

'Sammy,' Esther began slowly, 'if Ah was wantin' tae mairry you Ah would not only be a certified trader in gold, Ah would be jist certified period.'

Sammy's jaw dropped. 'Is that a naw?' he said.

'It's a naw-naw,' Esther said. 'Besides, whit aboot ma faith?'

'Ye could always get plastic surgery,' Sammy said.

'Whit's that got tae dae wi' ma faith?' Esther snapped.

'Ah beg yer pardon,' Sammy said, 'Ah thought ye said yer *face*.'

'Ye know Ah'm Jewish?' Esther said.

'So was Albert Einstein,' Sammy said. 'In fact ye look a bit like him, so ye dae.'

'That's no' nice, Sammy,' Aggie interrupted.

'Ah mean it in a nice wey,' Sammy said. 'He was a genius – jist like you are, Mrs Goldblum. Except you ur a genius for makin' money. Ah don't care whit anybody's religion is or whether they ur black, yella, brown or even green although Ah *would* prefer blue.'

'Is that a fact?' Esther said.

'Indubitably,' Sammy said, delighted to show his knowledge of the English language. Although he had only heard the word from a criminal lawyer who answered him when he asked if he thought he would get a jail term for house-breaking.

'In fact,' Sammy continued, 'Ah was once proposed marriage by a muslim. But turned the proposal doon.'

'Oh. Why was that?' Esther was intrigued.

'It was nothin' for tae dae wi' religion,' Sammy said. 'Ah am the maist unbiased man in Glesca, so Ah am.'

'So why turn the proposal doon?' Aggie was also intrigued.

'Ah didnae fancy him,' Sammy said without a smile.

'Ah think ye're a blawhard,' Esther said.

' Ah admit Ah do have a flatulence problem,' Sammy said. 'But that has nothin' for to do wi' ma unbigotedness. In fact Ah was also wance nearly married tae a lassie who was as black as the Ace of Spades.'

'Was she African?' Esther asked.

'Naw she was manky,' Sammy said.

'Aye, well, ma Jacob would turn in his grave if he thought that Ah'd give ma heart tae another,' Esther said.

'Whit would he say if ye gave yer bankbook?' Sammy grinned.

'Esther's late husband was a rabbit,' Sammy,' Aggie said.

'A *Rabbi*!' Esther corrected.

'Aye, wan o' them,' Aggie said, ' it's somethin' like a priest only they they ur no' obliged for to be celebrate.'

'Just like us here this night?' Sammy said, 'Geez, there's only three of us.'

'Aye, well, er – Nancy wull be in shortly,' Aggie said. 'Noo, c'mon, sit doon at the table. It's aboot time we got this celebration on the road.' She steered Sammy to a dining chair and placed him at the table. Esther rose and took a chair opposite.

But Aggie understood Sammy's questioning? Celebrations, especially golden wedding ones, depended on lots of happy people, the clinking of glasses, happy chatter, singing and lots of loud laughter and noise. The only noise attributed here would be the sound of Harry turning in his urn.

Still, she thought, Esther was here. Sammy was here and she was here. The vindaloos were here and there was still time for others to turn up. She was sorry that Alice couldn't stay but chiropractice was very important and if nobody turned up to practice where would the church's singers be? And Alice *was* a God-fearing woman. Well she was as a little girl. Her father was a grand master in the Orange Lodge and her mother was big in the Order of the Eastern Star. In fact her mother was big all over. And her mother, affectionately known in the street, as Clatty Mattie, was absolutely shocked when Alice, one day, told her that she wanted to become a nun.

She was stunned and surprised that Alice had come out with this blasphemous mouthful as Alice was just ten-weeks old. She immediately purchased a new pram – one with a hood so that she could take Alice out on rainy days.

Aggie saw that her two guests were settled in their seats and was hurrying through to the kitchen to prepare the vindaloos.

'So, ye were sayin' yer man was a rabbit, eh?' Sammy said, pulling in his chair.

'A *Rabbi*,' Aggie corrected .

'Oh. Aye,' Sammy said. 'Was he . . . er . . . was he in showbusiness?' he asked.

'Whit makes ye think that?' Esther said.

'A loat o' rabbis go in tae showbusiness,' Sammy said, 'That Jackie Mason for instance. He's a rabbi and he became a comedian – him frae Brookside.'

'Brooklyn,' Esther said, 'he comes frae Brooklyn – and he's no' as good a comedian as you,' she added acidly.

'Ah can never understaun' a word he says,' Sammy said, letting Esther's remark go.

'Ah canny understaun a word *you* say,' Esther said.

'Listen, Ah took electrocution lesssons and was voted the best English speaker in the class. Mind ye the rest o' the weans in ma class a' spoke Swahili. Ah could never understaun' that,' Sammy shook his head, puzzled.

'How as that?' Esther asked.

'They a' came frae Govan,' Sammy said.

'So, whit other rabbis dae ye know that are in showbusiness?' Esther asked, with interest.

'Him that sings that daft song wi' Knickers Kid-on, ye know the wan Ah mean.' Sammy began to sing, "Ah know Ah'm sittin' on the chair while you are sittin' on the flair jist gazin' at me" somethin' stupit' him – Rabbi Williams.'

'It's *Robbie* Sammy – *Robbie* Williams,' Aggie corrected.

Esther shook her head in despair. She felt her Jacob's name was being taken in vain.

'Ah've never heard so much rubbish as you're talkin',' she said to Sammy. 'Ma Jacob,' she dabbed her eye, 'may God rest his soul, didnae start oot in life to be a rabbi. He started aff in the garment trade wi' some needle and threed and wan button and it grew frae there,' she said proudly. 'Soon he had two buttons. Jacob put the word "waste" in waistcoat, the word "nick" in knickers and the word "dung" in dungarees. He was a clever man!' Esther dabbed her eye once more.

'So how come he went intac the jewellery gemme?' Sammy said.

'It was a night he went tae the pictures and seen the *Ten Commandments*,' Esther said. 'Wan look at Charleton Heston as Moses staggerin' doon that mountain side cairryin' they two big slabs of rock put a glint in his eye and convinced him.'

'He decided there an' then tae devote himsel' tae religion, tae the word of God?' Sammy said.

'Naw, the world of Gold,' Esther said. 'He saw them a' dancin' an' prancin' roon that golden calf and that made his mind up. If ye canny beat them, join them. Know whit he did?'

'Took dancin' lessons?' Sammy asked.

'Ye've heard o' the Great Bullion Robbery?' Esther asked.

'Oh. Aye. 'Sammy said with a faraway look. 'Ah only wished Ah'd been in on that – don't tell me your Jacob was in on it?'

'He masterminded it,' Esther said. 'And that's whit gave him the capital for to start up his jewellery business, first wi' a stall at the Barras oot in Kent Street and then inside oot o' the rain.'

'Imagine that!' Sammy said in awe.

'Aye, that's a lot o' bullion,' Esther said, winking at Aggie. Aggie smiled.

'Jacob got hisel' a good wife, tae,' she said, adding, 'you never got yersel' a wife, did ye Sammy? Could ye no' get a good lookin' young wumman tae look at ye?'

'Ah couldnae get an ugly *auld* wumman tae look at me,' Sammy said.

'Well, maybe wan o' these days ye'll find yersel' jist walkin' doon the street when suddenly – *Wham, Bam, Allikazam* – a wee stoater wull pass and yer eyes wull meet and before ye know it ye'll have hauf-a-dozen weans and a wee wifie runnin' efter ye,' Esther said.

'It'll be a chinge frae the polis runnin' efter him,' Aggie said.

Sammy shook his head. 'Naw, wi' ma luck,' he said, 'she'll be a candidate in the Miss Quasimodo competition. And the weans'll be dwarfs lookin' for a soft touch.'

'And there's naebody mair saft than you,' Esther said.

'Could ye never look on me romantically, Esther?' Sammy said softly.

'Ah couldnae even look at you rheumatically,' Esther said.

'C'mon noo,' Aggie said, 'time for to eat.' She made sure her two guests were comfortably seated at the table and turned towards the kitchen to prepare the Indian delicacy when a loud, authoritative knocking at the door stopped her in her tracks.

A tall uniformed policeman stood there.

'Ah am lookin' for a man who has been seen enterin' this hoose cairryin' a large, bejewelled gold chain,' he said in a deep voice.

Aggie saw it was pointless denying it and invited him in. The policeman's and Sammy's eyes met and the constable's eyes narrowed.

'You fit the description,' he said.

'Ye mean the man you ur lookin' for is a Brad Pitt look-a-like?' Sammy said.

'He is wee nyaff look-a-like,' the policeman said, 'and Ah hiv reason for to believe that you ur the said culprit.'

'Ah've never seen such a fuss ower a lavvy chain,' Aggie said.

'This, madam is nut a lavvy chain but wan that hings roon' yer neck.'

The policeman's eyes went to Sammy's feet where he had dropped the chain and had tried to kick it out of sight under the table.

'Ah ha!' the policeman gave a triumphant cry, stooping down and retrieving the gold chain.

'The evidence,' he cried.

'Whit evidence?' Sammy protested.

'Is this a lump of string wot I'm holding in my hand?' the cop said.

'It is not,' Sammy agreed. 'You ur holdin' in your massive mit the chain of ma authority.'

The policeman narrowed his eyes.

'The only authority this chain holds is the office of Lord Provost of Glesca who happened for to be wearin' it earlier on whilst doing his constitutional in George Square.'

The burly officer of the law coughed, wiped his mouth with a blue handkerchief and continued.

'His walk around the square was halted when he was approached by a man – described by a man accompanied wi' a Labrador – as a *wee nyaff* who proceeded for to relieve said honorable Lord Provost of said chain of office.'

Sammy looked aghast. 'Dae you think for wan moment that I – *me* – would stoop to such a felonious act as for to relieve our honorable Lord Provost – Glasgow's first citizen – of his mark of authority?' Sammy was hurt.

'Sammy widnae dae that,' Aggie volunteered.

Esther too, jumped to Sammy's defence. 'Listen constable,' she said, 'this man is a respected doctor – one of Scotland's leading plastic surgeons and I am one of his patients.'

The policeman bent forward towards Esther until their noses were almost touching.

'Has he been on strike?' he said facetiously?

'That is *nut* nice,' Sammy said.

'This chain,' Sammy said, 'was presented to me by my granny who is a hundred and forty-two years auld.'

The policeman's eyes brightened and Sammy noticed the sudden glint. 'And you might have a granny of similar age, eh?' Sammy added.

He followed this up by rolling up his trouser leg, putting his thumb to his nose and sticking out his tongue.

The cop immediately did the same, saying, 'Ma granny is only a wean of ninety-two.' Suddenly he was all apologies. 'Whit a dreadful mistake that Ah have made,' he said, pumping Sammy's hand. 'The Lord Provost was just oot for a wee donnar when this terrible deed happened. And when the man wi' the dug said he saw a wee nyaff runnin' away wi' the chain and a report came in ower ma personal hi-fi that a wee nyaff was seen enterin' this hoose cairryin' a gold chain, Ah immediately came tae the erroneous conclusion that the thief must be in this hoose.'

'An understandable confusion good sir,' said Sammy.

'However,' the cop went on, 'as Ah have already reported the entire incident Ah wull have for to ask you to accompany me tae the polis station for to see the sergeant and get this matter cleared up.'

Aggie threw up her hands – another guest taking off!

'Aw, naw!' she cried.

Sammy turned to Aggie and shrugged. 'Sorry, hen,' he said.

The cop crooked his arm which Sammy took as they headed towards the door.

'Don't worry,' the policeman said, 'the sergeant's granny is two-hunner and seventy.'

He looked Sammy straight in the eye and winked. Aggie flopped down on to a chair and sighed as they walked, arm-in-arm through the door. The only thing missing was the Laurel and Hardy signature tune.

'Well, that's that!' Aggie said. 'Thank God I've still got you here, Esther.'

Esther smiled. 'Twinty-four carat, hen.'

Aggie poured out two more glasses.

'So, whit aboot the grub?' Esther said, rubbing her hands.

'Right!' Aggie said, jumping to her feet. 'We'll celebrate

together, Esther. But where *is* Nancy?' a worried looked crossed her face. 'Ah jist hope that stalker hisnae caught up wi' her.'

Aggie gave Esther a napkin and saw that it was well tucked in under her friend's chins.

'Get ready for a feast, hen,' Aggie said.

Suddenly the telephone rang.

'Oh. It might be Nancy!' Aggie said hopefully reaching for the handset.

Esther tucked the napkin down deeper into her cleavage and heard Aggie saying, 'Aye, she's here – hang on.' 'It's for you, Esther,' she said, handing over the phone.

Aggie left Esther talking and hurried into the kitchen. The vindaloos were ready and Aggie, grimacing, took two from the microwave oven.

She wondered what Harry saw in this pungent grub from the Punjab? The strong aroma wafted across the kitchen and the smell reminded her of Harry's breath. She held the tray at arms length as she entered the room and placed the meal on the table. Esther was still talking on the phone.

'Yes,' she was saying, 'Oh, no! Don't tell me . . . '

Aggie's ears went up. Obviously bad news. Poor Esther, she thought, getting bad news just before getting stuck into her vindaloo. It couldn't be anything that had happened to Jacob for he was dead and nothing worse than that could happen to him. She tried to look as though she weren't listening to her friend's conversation and sat down and began to pick at her plate.

'Aye, okay,' Esther said. 'Aye – right away,' she hung up.

'Somethin' wrang, hen?' said Aggie said.

Esther puckered her lip. 'Aw, Ah'm awfu' sorry Aggie,' she said, 'Ah hiv tae go – it's an emergency – Ruebin.'

'Hymie,' Aggie corrected, 'He's no' deid, is he?'

'He might as well be,' Esther said. 'He's taken wan o' his daft fits. He takes them noo and again. It a' began efter his faither died. Ah wanted him tae be buried on Mount Sinai like a' good Jews want. Ruebin wisnae very pleased and said we didnae have for to go a' that distance and Ah tried tae explain tae him that it was his faither's wish that he be buried on a good Jewish mountain.'

'Aw, he should've listened tae whit his faither wanted,' Aggie said. 'Of coorse sometimes ye just canny get whit ye want. Ma Harry wanted tae be taken tae a taxidermist when he died like Roy Rogers' hoarse Trigger, but the taxidermist refused Harry's written doon wish.'

'Whit reason did he give?' Esther asked.

'He only did dugs and cats an' that, he said, and besides, he didnae work in sage an' onion.' Aggie chuckled, 'Aye,' she said, 'ma Harry loved his wee laugh.'

'Aye, well Ah wish Ah could laugh,' Esther said.

'Aye . . . er . . . Rueb . . . er . . . Hymie didnae want for to go to Jerusalem tae bury his faither on a good Jewish mountain?' Aggie said with sympathy.

'He said there was good Jewish mountains here, in Scotland,' Esther said.

'Ah never knew that,' Aggie said.

'Ah asked him tae name them,' Esther said.

'And did he?' Aggie asked.

'Oh aye,' Esther said, 'his favourite wans Benjamin Lomond.'

'Ah never knew Ben Lomond was a Jewish mountain,' Aggie said.

'Naebody did,' Esther said, 'only ma Ruebin.'

'Hymie,' Aggie corrected.

'Aye, him,' Esther said. 'His heid's away wi' it, so it is. Ah'm really worried aboot him, so Ah am. Noo he's taken another wan o' his turns. That was a call frae ma next door neighbour.'

'Whit's the trouble?' Aggie asked, concerned.

'Rue . . . er . . . Hymie is oot in the middle o' the street preachin'. He' bawlin' that's he's a born-again Christian.'

'Aw, that's nice!' Aggie said.

'How can it be nice', Esther snapped, 'when his uncle's a rabbi?'

'Ah wonder whit brought this oan?' Aggie said.

'Ah should've noticed somethin' was wrang ages ago,' Esther said, 'when Ah noticed that he was wearin' his coaller back tae front.'

'Ach, that disnae mean anythin',' Aggie said, 'loats o' boys dae that.'

'But no' wi' their tie and jaicket as well,' Esther said.

'No' only would he no'know if he was comin' or goin' but you don't know if *you're* comin' or goin', hen,' Aggie commiserated.

'Noo he's shoutin' that he wants tae enter the catholic church and join a religious order. *That* is unforgivable,' Esther dabbed her eye – the left one.

'Ye – ye – ye mean he wants tae become a priest?' Aggie stammered.

'Worse,' Esther said, 'a *nun!*'

'That Julie Andrews has a loat tae answer for,' Aggie said.

'So ye see, Aggie, Ah'll really hiv tae go before he gets cerried away wi' himsel'.'

'Aye, he might get cerried away right enough,' Aggie said.

'Ah'm sorry, hen, tae leave ye on yer anniversary,' Esther said, pecking Aggie on the cheek and hurrying towards the door. She gave a weak wave, dabbed her eye – her right one and was gone.

Aggie slumped on to the easy chair and sighed. Her eyes went over to Harry's photo and she sighed even more deeply.

'Aw, Harry,' she said sadly, 'it's a' fa'in' tae bits. There's naebody here and Ah don't even know whit's happened tae Nancy. It's jist me, your photay and two dozen Edwinas.'

She got up and went over to the window. Pulling back the curtain, she peered out. A stray dog cocked its leg by the street lamp and a police car screamed past klaxon blazing. The dog took fright and abandoned its ritual and yelping, raced half-cocked down the street and vanished round the corner.

Aggie sighed once again. Even that wee dug didnae get a chance tae dae whit it set oot tae dae, she thought and shaking her head sadly, returned to her chair, flopped down and closed her eyes – both of them.

A loud rapping at the door made her jump. *Nancy* was the first thought that came into her mind. She's forgotten her keys. Aggie hurried to the door and threw it wide open.

A tall, skinny man with a grey goatee beard stood there and by his side an elegant lady with a silver fox fur slung round her shoulders.

It had to be Wee Dumpy McNab her classmate from way back. Aggie always knew that Wee Dumpy would do well. She had that something about her. When the class of eight year olds was asked by Miss McLaughlin their teacher, to bring out their pennies for their morning milk, Wee Dumpy brought out her cheque book.

Her clothes were the envy of all the other little girls. She was the only girl who had her school uniform made-to-measure – in mohair, Dumpy swore the material came from a real mo. Still, Aggie was delighted to see her. She wondered who the skinny man could be? Surely not her father? Aggie remembered Dumpy's father as a squat little man who wore a rug on his head – Axminster it was.

'Come away in – come in,' Aggie cried, ushering them into the room and steering them towards two chairs.

'Well, noo, it's good tae see ye, Dumpy,' she said, 'Ah would never hiv recognised ye – ye've chinged that much.'

'Oh, in what way?' Dumpy said.

'Well, ye're nose used tae be a loat bigger for a start. Hiv ye had a nose job?'

'What are you talking about?' the skinny man snapped. 'Don't you know who you are addressing?'

'Ah am talkin' tae wee Dumpy here,' Aggie said, and pointing her thumb towards the man, said, 'who's Wurzel, here?'

The man spluttered. 'What do you mean?' he snapped, 'I am this lady's agent. My name is Hector McSorley.'

'Agent for whit?' Aggie said, 'Ur youse goin' roon' sellin' fitba' coupons?'

The man spluttered even more. '*Football coupons?*' he cried. 'How dare you. Do you not recognise this lady from your television screen and top women's magazines?'

'Dumpy here?' Aggie said bringing down her brow.

'I'll let you know that this is Miss Dumpy Laverne – er – Miss Chu Chu Laverne.' He quickly corrected himself, adding, 'the famous super model.'

'Oh! Ah beg yer pardon,' Aggie said, very impressed. 'But that's no' yer real name, is it? Ah mean Chu Chu – whit kinda name is that – called efter a train.'

'Many people who are in a profession that's in the public eye change their name,' Hector said.

'Only when ye get merried,' Aggie said.

'No. no,' Hector said. 'Look at Marion Morrison for instance.'

'Never heard o' her,' Aggie said.

'Marion Morrison started off on the silver screen as Singing Sandy – you've never heard of Singing Sandy?' Hector shook his head.

'If Marion Morrison chinged her name tae Singin' Sandy it must've been mair than her name she chinged,' Aggie said.

'Marion Morrison became John Wayne,' Hector said. 'He had to, didn't he? You couldn't have this big, six-foot-four cowboy riding the range and catching the bad guys with a name like Marion Morrison, could you?'

'Ah don't know,' Aggie said, 'the baddies might've died laughin'.'

'It's a common practice in showbusiness.' Hector went on. 'Doris Kapplehoff became Doris Day, Reginald Dwight became Elton John, Arlington Brough became Robert Taylor – I could go on and on.'

'Aye, but callin' yersel efter Thomas the Tank Engine, that's goin' a bit faur. Chu Chu! Ah've never heard anythin' so daft. Ma faither would've turned, laughin' in his grave if he had heard that, so he would've.' Aggie chuckled.

'What was your father's name?' Hector asked.

'Waverley,' Aggie said.

'After Sir Walter Scott's epic works?' Hector said.

'Efter a steamboat,' Aggie said, 'Ma maw gave him that name.'

'Because she a great Walter Scotts admirer?' Hector asked

'Because he was always steamin',' Aggie said.

Chu Chu Laverne sat stroking her fox fur and looking bored.

'Would youse like a wee cuppa tea?' Aggie said.

'No thank you,' Chu Chu said.

'Whit aboot yer dug there?' Aggie said. 'Would it like a bowl o' Bounce?'

'Oh you have a dog yourself. Do you?' the model said.

'Naw, but Ah could gie it some vindaloo – that would make it bounce.'

'Anyway,' Chu Chu went on. 'this is not a dog I have. It's a silver fox fur.'

'Huh!' Aggie said. standing straight and folding her arms. 'So ye've got high an' mighty hiv ye? Wan o' them country-wide wallahs? Chasin' they poor wee foxes a' ower the place wi' big, snarlin' dugs.'

'This fox fur let me tell you came from *Jenners* department store,' Chu Chu said haughtily.

'Geez, ye're even chasin' thcm intae shoaps noo,' Aggie said.

'You are talking rubbish,' Chu Chu said.

'Ye always wur a bit of a snob,' Aggie said. 'And look at ye noo. Ye've get mair paint on yer face than the Forth Bridge. And Chu Chu . . . ? My God, whit a name!'

'It's French,' Hector said. 'It's good for her image.'

'*Image*!' Aggie cried. 'Whit image? You ur behind a' this. Ye've turned that lassie's heid, so ye hiv. Look at her face. She has obviously had plastic surgery done on her coupon by a doactor who's got the hippy-hippy shakes.'

'That is scandalous,' Hector blurted.

'And jist look at her nose – look at it,' Aggie said, pointing a shaking finger at her friend's face.

'And what's wrong with it?' Hector said huffily. 'It looks just like any other nose.'

'Aye, but it should be above her mooth no' under her ear.' Aggie snapped.

'Och, you're havering,' Hector said.

Aggie looked at Hector with grave suspicion. 'Who ur you anyway?' she said, narrowing her eyes.

'I told you,' Hector said, 'I'm Miss Laverne's agent.'

Chu Chu nodded. 'He's a Svengali,' she said.

'Ah don't care whit religion he is,' Aggie said, 'It seems tae me that he has got too much say in your life, Dumpy.'

'Her name is Chu Chu,' Hector said. 'The most glamorous super model in Britain.'

Chu Chu sighed, breathed on her long, scarlet nails and polished them on her fox fur. She did the same, removing her teeth and replacing them. She smiled and got up,wandering over to the sideboard where she picked up a photo of soldiers wearing the tartan of the Royal Horse Dung Regiment and with a yawning camel standing behind them.

78

'A fine bunch of men!' she said, turning to Aggie. 'Your husband in this group?'

Aggie nodded. 'He was a soldier – a Scottish soldier, who wandered far away,' Aggie said, stopping herself from bursting into song.

'Is he the one in the pith helmet?' Chu Chu asked.

'He *did* use it for that purpose wance or twice,' Aggie said.

'Have you no children?' Chu Chu asked, replacing the picture.

'Oh aye,' Aggie said. 'Ah've got ma daughter, Nancy. We *did* hiv another wee lassie, Rosey, but we loast her.'

'Oh. I am sorry,' Chu Chu said. 'You had no more?'

Aggie shook her head. 'Naw, Harry thought two was enough. He said a' new weans looked like Winstion Churchill – especially oor Nancy.'

'What a terrible thing to say,' Chu Chu said.

'Aye, he used tae look at her lyin' there in her pram and shake his heid sayin' she was the spittin' image o' Mr Churchill.'

'Did that not make you angry?'

'It did.' Aggie said, 'Ah mean the wean did him nae herm. She was jist lyin there quite content smokin' her cigar.'

'The baby smoked a cigar?' Chu Chu cried.

'She didnae like dummy tits,' Aggie said.

Chu Chu and Hector glanced at each other and smiled.

'I didn't recognise your Willie at first,' Chu Chu said.

'Who's Wullie?' Aggie said, puzzled.

'Why, your husband, of course,' Chu Chu said.

'Wullie?' Aggie frowned.

'He was much taller as I remember,' Chu Chu said, 'with shocking red hair.'

'Ma man had a shockin' red face.' Aggie said. 'Never shockin' red hair. Even when his face wisnae red it was still shockin'.'

'Wasn't your Willie the big man on points at Bridgeton Cross?' Chu Chu said.

'Ma man was on *pints* but never *points*,' Aggie said. 'Listen Dumpy, ma man's name is nut Wullie it's *Harry!*'

'And *her* name is not Dumpy, it's Chu Chu.' Hector said.

'You urnae wee Dumpy McNab who was in ma class at school?' Aggie asked.

79

'Naw, ma name's Bella Maguire,' Chu Chu said, forgetting her posh accent for a moment.

'Otherwise known throughout the world as Chu Chu Laverne,' Hector was quick to point out.

'Ye – ye – mean youse are no' here for to celebrate ma golden weddin' anniversary?' Aggie said, disappointed.

'Ah must've comed tae the wrang door,' Chu Chu said. 'Ah came for to pey a visit tae ma auld freen', Annie McLatchie, who Ah hivnae seen for years. Is this no' number twenty-five?'

'Twinty-seven, hen.' Aggie said. 'Annie McLatchie lives in the hoose next door. Jist follow yer nose, if it still works, ye canny miss the smell.'

'Oh. Good!' Chu Chu said, 'Ah hivnae loast ma auld pal, then?'

'Naw, a' you've loast is yer accent,' Aggie said.

'Ah thought ye didnae look like Annie,' Chu Chu said.

'Aye, and you didnae really look like wee Dumpy,' Aggie said.

'We baith made a mistake then,' Chu Chu said, heading for the door.

Aggie dashed after Hector and Chu Chu. 'Ye're very welcome tae stey,' she said with a plea. 'Aah'd be gled o' yer company. Whit ye say, eh?'

'Ah'm sorry, Hen,' Chu Chu said, 'but Ah hivnae seen ma auld pal for donkeys and she knows we're comin.'

'Aw, can Ah no' beg ye?' Aggie said.

'Come, Chu Chu,' Hector said, tugging at his client's sleeve. 'We have no time for chit-chat.'

'Sorry, hen,' Chu Chu said, 'but Ah hope ye have a happy anniversary – you and your man.'

Chu Chu closed the door behind her.

Aggie sighed. 'Me and ma man?' She stopped the tear running down her cheek with the corner of the table cloth.

CHAPTER THREE

AGGIE SAT BROODING FOR A WHILE AND THEN AS THOUGH HIT BY a bolt of lightning, jumped to her feet. If the mountain would not come to Mohammet then Mohammet would go to the mountain. Rising, she put on her coat and quickly scrawled a note for Nancy, should she turn up and was not lying mugged somewhere. 'Will be back shortly,' the note said – and off she went.

Annie McLatchie in person opened the door. 'So, whit is it?' she snapped.

Aggie took a deep breath. Annie McLatchie, as far as Aggie was concerned, was the original Neighbour from Hell. All television programmes with that title were based on Annie McLatchie. Aggie was sure of that. Often, Aggie had complained to the council about the loud music blasting out of the McLatchie living room but nothing had been done about it. Many a night's sleep had been lost by Aggie and Harry. In fact the whole street shook and her doctor had prescribed an annual prescription of Valium Extra. That was ordinary Valium supplied with a brochure for coffins. Even during Harry's wake the music blasted out at fever pitch. It was so loud that even Harry sat up, fingers in ears. Nothing was done and the Scottish Symphony Orchestra continued to rehearse in the McLatchie household.

Annie McLatchie was known as Manky Annie. She could do an Al Jolson act at the local pub without make-up. People took an instant dislike to her and once when she went to church she was mugged by the priest. It was said that once, after hearing her confession, the priest committed suicide.

Aggie could not believe that here she was standing at Manky Annie's door. She let the obvious hostile greeting pass. Clearing her throat, she began, 'Er – Mrs McLatchie —'

'Whit is it?' Annie snarled.

'Ah – er – know ye've got visitors,' Aggie said, 'But Ah was wonderin' if youse would like for tae come in tae ma hoose. Ah'm celebratin' ma Golden Weddin' Anniversary.'

Annie's eyes narrowed. 'You've a bloody cheek askin' me that,' she said, her face twisted, 'efter a' the trouble you've gave me.'

Aggie tried to keep calm and her arms straight down by her side, her fists clenched tightly.

'Ur ye sayin' *naw*?'

'Ye're jist a troublemaker and anyway, how can ye hiv a golden weddin' anniversary when yer man's deid an' buried?'

Aggie couldn't contain herself. Who was *she* to mention Harry's sacred name? 'You waash yer mooth oot,' Aggie snapped. 'You've a cheek for tae call *me* a troublemaker – you that lets yer weans run riot.'

'Whit dae ye mean?' Annie said narrowing her eyes.

'They're the wildest, noisiest boys in the street,' Aggie said, 'A' hell breaks loose when they go oot. Auld Mister Campbell was rushed tae hospital wan day last week jist minutes efter your boys took tae the street playin' cowboys an' Indians.'

Annie McLatchie shrugged. 'So whit has that tae dae wi' ma boys?' she said.

'His hearin' aid blew up,' Aggie said.

'A' wee boys play cowboys an' Indians,' Annie said.

'No' wi' real guns they don't,' Aggie snapped.

'Aye, well, ye're wastin' yer time comin' tae ma door. Me an' ma freen's have nae wish for tae celebrate your daft anniversary. Besides, we've got tickets for the Pavilion pantomime and that's where we're goin'.'

'They'll need tae fumigate the theatre efter you leave,' Aggie said.

'Ur you suggestin' Ahm no' clean?' Annie snarled.

'Ah'm telt that when ye went doon tae Madame Wee Nellie's tae get yer hair done, she had tae use a blow lamp and she had tae shut the shoap for a week and bring in the environmental department.'

'That's no' true,' Annie said.

'Aye, it's true a'right,' Aggie said. 'Can ye no' take a hint?'

'Whit hint's that?' Annie said.

'That day the cleansin' Department lorry came roon tae collect yer wheelie bin. They took away the bin an' left the lorry.'

'Away ye go an' bile yer heid,' Annie snapped.

'Look at yer gairden,' Aggie said, 'it's a jungle so it is and Ah'm sure that's cannabis ye're growin in that coarner.'

'You mind yer ain business,' Annie McLatchie said, her face flushing slightly.

'Aye, that's cannabis a'right, Ah'm sure o' it.' Aggie was on her high horse.

'Oh, and ur you a forensic scientist, ur ye?' Annie snapped back.

'Ye don't need for to be a fornicatin' scientist tae spot that,' Aggie said.

'Oh, and how come?' Annie said, folding her arms.

'Ah was lookin' oot ma windae wan day and Ah saw a wee dug chewin' on that plant,' Aggie said tightening her lip.

'Whit aboot it,' Annie said.

'The next time Ah saw that wee dug it had distemper.'

'Ach, loats o' wee dugs take distemper,' Annie retorted.

'It had paint and wallpaper as well and was decoratin' its kennel,' Aggie said.

'Ah don't believe it,' Annie snapped.

'Ah should've reported you to the RSPCA,' Aggie said. 'And another thing. If that plant isnae cannabis how come ye've got the queerist wee birds in the street? Ah've seen squadrons o' them – wee sparras peckin' away at it. Then they sit up on that tree and sing their wee lungs oot a' night – no' jist yer ordinary chirpin – a whole line up o' them was up there wan night and gave a lovely rendition o' *The Nuns Chorus*. That plant is affectin' them.'

'Don't talk rubbish,' Annie said.

'Rubbish, is it?' Aggie said. 'Listen, hen, Ah saw a wee robin redbreast up there singin' for a' its worth *Ahm Dreamin' of a White Christmas*.'

'Ah've never heard such twaddle in ma life,' Annie said.

'Yer hoose is like a pigsty. Mice a' ower the place.'

'Don't gie me that,' Annie sneered, *You've* got mice. It's rampant around here.'

'Ah, but Ah've got *white* mice. Nane o' yer scruffy brownies runnin' aboot *ma* hoose,' Aggie said.

'Ah'm surprised at masel' staunin' here talkin' tae you, so Ah am,' Annie said, screwing up her nose.

'Ah'm surprised that ye're staunin' – period,' Aggie said.

'Ur you suggestin' that Ah take a drink?' Annie said tightening her lips.

'Ah'm suggestin' nuthin',' Aggie said. 'Ah'm telling ye straight. Never a night passes when Ah don't hear ye staggerin' up the path singin' yer hert oot.'

'Ah never sing comin' up the path,' Annie said.

'Well, it's either you singin' or yer cat's in a fight again. You, yer man, yer weans and yer cats should've been evicted years ago. Youse are definitely neighbours frae hell – although Ah think the Devil himsel' widnae stey wi' ye.'

'At least Ah've no'got a coaffin outside ma windae,' Annie said.

'There's nae herm hivin' a coaffin ootside yer windae as long as there's naebody in it,' Aggie said. 'A' that is in that coaffin is the good earth an some marras.'

'So you say,' Annie replied.

'Ye don't think ma Harry's in it dae ye?' Aggie snapped back.

'Ah widnae put it past ye,' Annie said, 'he was always hingin' oot the windae – takin' everythin' in – nosey parker that he was.'

'Ma Harry was *nut* a nosey parker,' Aggie said angrily. 'He was an obverver of life. He loved studyin'people, so he did.'

'Aye, lassies maistly,' Annie sneered.

'Harry kept himsel' to himsel',' Aggie said. 'He was never in trouble wi' the polis and gied me his wages every week, so he did. Your family is never oot o' trouble. The polis motor, wi' sirens blarin', is never away frae your door. It's there mair times than the ice-cream van.'

Aggie was on her high horse. Anybody who dared take Harry's name in vain was asking for her wrath.

'Ice-cream van?' Annie said, 'ye're talkin' tripe.'

'Tripe, am Ah?' Aggie said. 'Listen, the cops are that embarrassed wi' weans comin' up tae them askin' for a pokey hat that they've chinged their sirens frae *nee-naw*, *nee-naw* tae *Popeye the sailorman*. And maist o' the time they're here it's because o' your boy – he's the school bully.'

'Ma wee Saddam?' Annie snapped. 'He's the dux o' the school. So he is. He's got ten a-levels.'

'Spirit levels, ye mean,' Aggie said, 'when other weans stey aff school sufferin' wi' a cauld, he steys aff sufferin' wi' a hangover. Him only eight-year-auld, tae. Of coorse he learns it at hame.'

A voice from inside the house bawled, 'Comin' in Annie? Yer Guinness is losin' its heid.'

'An' so am Ah,' Annie replied.

'Ye'd better get in,' Aggie said, 'that's Chu-chu gettin' steam up in there. So, ye ur no' interested in ma celebrations, then?'

'Ah am whit,' Annie said, 'and don't come tae ma door again.' With that she slammed the door shut.

Aggie took a paper hankie from her pocket and gingerly pushed open the letter box. Peering in, she shouted, 'Ah widnae touch your door wi' a ten-foot barge pole. Ah had tae say a quick prayer before Ah put ma haun's on yer manky letterbox,' Aggie yelled.

'There's nothin' manky aboot ma letterbox,' Annie yelled back.

'O, naw?' Aggie bawled, 'oor postman put a letter in it last week and when he took his haun' oot he had rabies.'

'Ah hivnae got a dug,' Annie yelled back.

'Exactly!' Aggie said.

Aggie walked slowly down the path. Even to go to Annie's door was an ordeal but she was willing to let bygones be bygones and would have welcomed Annie and her visitors in to help celebrate her very special day. She wondered what Harry would have thought? Harry was not one to hold grudges. It took him all his time to hold his liquor. But Annie had declined her invitation and so the war would go on.

Shame! Annie could've been so much different. She had a nice smile. Aggie knew that for Annie pawned it every Tuesday. Something must have turned her sour. But what?

Perhaps it was the fact that her marriage had broken down.

Her man, Osama, broke her heart when he fell for a mud wrestler. And when she tackled him about it he broke her jaw as well. Not only that the mud wrestler, who was an extremely jealous individual, challenged her to a bout and she felt she had to prove to herself to Osama, that she was someone to be reckoned with. But her legs shook as she climbed into that ring and faced this large, hairy brute and she suddenly wondered why Osama would throw her over for this – this person. Soon she was being thrown over again by the hairy monster who had stolen the heart of her dear husband. But she suddenly didn't care anymore. If that was Osama's taste she didn't want to know. The gorilla was billed as *Mary the Hairy* and had once worked in a circus as the bearded lady and doubling up as an elephant. This was no lady, though and was charged under the Trades Description Act. She was ordered to do two hundred hours community service which she did giving local children and pensioners rides on her back around Bridgeton.

Annie changed after Osama and Hairy Mary ran off to Zimbabwe where they set up a stall selling Mugabe dolls for fifty pence each – pins were extra.

Annie let herself go after that. From the prim, immaculately dressed, vivacious woman that she was she became morose, rude and from *Natty Annie* she became *Clatty Annie*. Her son, Saddam, had tried to be a worthy lad at the beginning of Annie's trip down the tubes. He was delighted when he won the Best Moustache Award at Blackpool. The judges were astounded as he strolled on to the platform and they had no hesitation in awarding him the coveted prize – a moustache shaving mug made in pewter. He was only five at the time.

But wee Saddam soon fell into his mother's ways and followed her down the tubes. Annie drove him mad by continually nagging him to make something of himself and was delighted one day when he arrived home after seeing the film, *Snow White and the Seven Dwarfs* and proclaimed that at last he had found his vocation. He wanted to go into show business. Walt Disney's brilliant masterpiece had inspired him. He insisted he wanted to be a dwarf and join a circus. Annie was devastated. She had just bought him a track suit that would fit Arnold Swarzenegger. So Wee Saddam ran away from home and joined a flea circus. The circus ringmaster welcomed him with open arms as he had brought from home many of its star attractions. Not only that the kindly ringmaster had promised that one day he *would* take to the sawdust as the circus's star dwarf attraction.

★ ★ ★

Aggie left Annie's door, riotous singing echoing in her ear. It was early yet – still time for her guests to arrive. She looked up into the evening sky. A big, amber moon shone and her mind went back to her courting days with Harry. She remembered them sitting on a bench in George Square and Harry pointed to that same moon.

'Someday, hen,' he said, 'Ah'm gonny gie you that.'

He never did and she was glad. They only had a single-end'.

The smell of fish and chips wafted across her path as she walked down London Road.

Big Mario Greenberg welcomed her with outstretched arms as she entered the shop. 'Aw, hello Mrs,' he cried, 'why you-a lookin' like-a somebody stole your-a scone. Eh?'

Aggie shook her head. 'Problems, Mario, problems,' Aggie repeated.

'Ach. We a' gotta problems,' the big man said, grimacing. 'So, whits-a-yours. eh?'

'It's ma golden weddin' anniversary,'Aggie said.

'And that's a problem?' Mario said, knitting his brows.

Aggie nodded. 'Aye,' she said, 'have you ever celebrated yer golden weddin' anniversary?'

'Only-a wance and that was enough,' Mario said. 'Fifty years o' misery, it-a was. We met at-a the grape-a tramplin' festival for the vino. The first dozen boattles went-a straight-a tae-a weddin in the toon and a' the-a guests drapped-a deid efter wan-a gless.'

'How was that?' Aggie asked.

'Her-a feet wur-a stinkin'. She had-a foot and-a mooth disease Ah think.'

'So, why did ye mairry her, then?' Aggie was curious.

'Her-a faither said Ah had-a dishonoured her. *Me* dishonour *her*!' Mario cried. 'She had a face like-a the back end of a camel and a nose like an elephant. Her-a faither jist-a wanted for tae mairry her oaff and he says he-a saw oor tootsies entwined in a provocative wey and that if Ah didnae-a walk his ugly daughter doon-a the aisle it widnae be the grapes that would-a be getttin' pulverised.' Mario looked dejected.

'So ye got married – ' Aggie did not get finishing the sentence.

'Fifty years of-a hell,' the big chippie interrupted.

'Aw, Ah canny say that. Harry and me hit it aff right frae the word go, so we did.'

'That's-a good,' Mario said, 'Whit-a did ye see in him that made ye like that?'

'He had a smile that stabbed ye right here, in the heart,' Aggie pointed to her chest.

'Because of his-a countenance, eh?' Mario said.

'Naw he had buck teeth,' Aggie said.

'And this is yer golden wedding anniversary, eh?' Mario said.

'It is – fifty years of bliss.'

'Your-a man was a heavy drinker, eh?' Mario added.

'No' really,' Aggie said.

'But-a you said you had-a fifty years of . . .'

Aggie interrupted him, '*Bliss!* Mario, *bliss!*'

'So where is this-a lucky man? He-a no' celebratin' as well?'

'He's deid,' Aggie said.

'Aw, that's a shame,' Mario said. 'Noo you're all alone, eh?'

'Naw, naw,' Aggie said.

'Whit are ye-a daein' oot when you should-a be celebratin'?'

''Hiv ye seens ma wee Nancy?' Aggie asked.

'Naw, you've always got yer claeths oan when ye come intae ma-a shoap.'

'Naw, Ah mean ma daughter, Nancy,' Aggie said. 'She left the hoose tae escort a wee wumman tae the bus stoap.'

'Oh, you've-a got for tae watch yersel' around here,' Mario said, shaking his head.

'Whit dae ye mean?' Aggie asked, screwing up her nose.

'Ma-a wife, Sophia – no' as in Sofia as in-a Sofia Loren,' Mario explained, 'but as in she's Sophi-a family o' gorillas.'

A smile flitted across Aggie's face.

'Anywey,' Mario continued, 'wan-a night she was a-walkin' doon the street, right-a outside ra shoap, when she was mugged.'

Aggie's hand went to her mouth. 'Oh, whit a shame!' she gasped.

'Anywey,' Mario went on, 'she staggered intae the shoap her two eyes blackend and puffed and her-a lips a' swelt and rubbery lookin'.'

'Oh, ye must've been devastated, Mario,'

'Naw, naw, Ah wis-a delighted – she-a looked better than she did when she went oot'

'Aw, Mario,' Aggie chuckled, 'Ah'm ashamed o' ye. Ah know ye don't mean that.'

'Who don't?' Mario said with a shrug. 'Listen, if Sophia –' He stopped, raised his eyes to heaven and murmered, 'Aw, it-a breaks ma-a heart tae mention that lovely name and think how it can-a mean the positive and the negative, a flower tae a flour bag,' he sighed before continuing. 'Aye, if that-a wumman who is ma-a wife, wisnae the-a daughter of the godfather.'

'Ye – ye mean Marlon Brando's her faither?' Aggie asked, her jaw dropping.

'Naw, naw,' Mario said, shaking his head, 'the *real* heid o' the family-a ruthless man who would have nae-a hesitation of puttin' oot-a contract oan me.'

'Ach, away wi' ye,' Aggie said, 'that's jist in the pictures.

'Ye-a think so?' Mario cried. 'Whit dae ye-a think happened tae that patriot that mugged her, eh?'

'Did the polis find him?' Aggie quizzed.

'They never did,' Mario said, 'He got a fish sent tae him.'

'Aw, that was nice,' Aggie said, is yer faither-in-law in the same gemme as you?'

'Mrs –' Mario explained, 'when-a ma faither-in-law sends you a fish it means that you wull-a soon be swimmin' wi' the fishes, so ye wull.'

'Nothin' nicer than a nice swim,' Aggie said.

'No' when ye're a wearin' concrete shoes, hen,' Mario said.

'So whit happened tae yer wife's mugger, then?' Aggie was all ears.

'He-a woke up wan-a moarnin' and found an ugly bloody deid-a hoarse's heid lying next tae him.'

'Oh my!' Aggie's hand went up to her mouth again.

'At first he-a thought he had-a gone too faur and thought it was ma-a Sophia that had a climbed in beside him.'

'So, where is he noo?' Aggie was interested in Mario's tale.

'Remember the-a Kingston Bridge began for tae-a lean tae the wan-a side?'

Aggie nodded.

'Who dae ye think is-a proppin. It up?'

'Ach, away wi' ye,' Aggie chuckled.

'Here-a noo,' Mario brightened up and changed the subject. 'This is your-a golden weddin, eh?'

Aggie sighed, 'Aye, and naebody's turned up tae celebrate wi' me.'

'Ach-a well,' Mario said, 'they're-a no' worth-a botherin' aboot so they're-a no'.'

'Aye, well, maybe you're right,' Aggie sighed.

'Here,' Mario cried, 'You can still-a celebrate. Your-a golden day and Ah should-a be gien' you a big-a golden cutlet, naw?'

Aggie smiled.

'But, seein' that Ah hiv-a nae golden cutlets, how aboot wan o' me, eh?'

'Whit's wan of you, Mario?' Aggie said, looking at him quizzically.

'A big-a haddy, eh?'

They both burst out laughing. 'Aw, Mario,' Aggie said, 'ye're a tonic, but naw thanks, son. Ah jist want tae find ma Nancy, At least two of us can celebrate oorsel's – unless you and Sophia would like to come, eh?'

Mario's mouth opened in water-melon grin, his teeth flashing.

'Ah'd love tae.' he said. Aggie brightened she wouldn't have to be alone. Harry was working well and God *was* good.

'Hey, Maria,' Mario bawled, 'come in-here. We're-a goin tae a party.'

Mario's buxom wife hurried in wiping her hands on her apron. 'We-a canny go-a naewhere,' she cried, 'Franco is comin' ower wi' the bambino tae prepare for his first holy communion in the moarnin'.' She crossed herself. Aggie's heart sank.

'Sorry hen,' Mario muttered, 'Ah forgot.'

'Well, Ah'd better get goin' and keep lookin'. Ma Nancy and Wee Alice could be lyin' in a coarner somewhere mugged.'

'It'll no' be by Sophia's mugger anyway,' Mario said.

'Naw, right enough,' Aggie said, 'he's too busy swimmin' wi' the fishes, eh?'

Aggie left the shop laughing. It would take a lot to lift the depression from her. She took in a deep breath of the evening air and headed down towards Bridgeton Cross. She remembered the tale from the Good Book when Jesus told of a man who had invited guests to a feast in his home and how nobody turned up giving all sorts of excuses, and of how angry he became and sent his servants out into the streets with the instructions to find the poor the blind and the crippled. Luke, chapter 14 verses 15-24 – yes, Aggie remembered her Sunday School days. So why not take a leaf from the Good Book?

The *Brigton Umbrella* was a good place to start, Aggie thought. Not really an umberella of the portable canvas type, but a famous landmark that stands, roof slated and on pillars with benches and public toilets underneath its dome – lavatories now blocked off, filled in and defunct. It was a great place for a rendevous. Pensioners gathered there, safe from the rain and wind and chatted about old times of Celtic and Rangers football teams and groused in general about the state of the world.

Aggie arrived at the umbrella and noticed a few old folk sitting there. Across the street was the Olympia Cinema – the poshest cinema in the east end. Its plush balcony seats were reserved for Saturday nights with your *lumber* and there were always queues outside. You stood in the rain, moving slowly down the queue and chatting oblivious of the weather.

Then you would hear some gallant chap, standing behind you with his girlfriend, saying, 'Ur ye hungry, hen?'

'Starvin!' She would reply and the next minute he was off to the wee chip shop in nearby Orr Street.

When he returned the greatest aroma in the world – that of fish and chips – wafted down the queue and seconds later the line-up thinned out as other chivalrous beaus hurried to satisfy the hunger of their drooling darlings. Aggie's eyes went over to the imposing, cream-tiled palace of dreams and memories flooded her mind. Of her and Harry queueing up, dripping wet and clinging to each other and laughing and joking. Harry, always conscious of his appearance, only laughed when he had his teeth in. She remembered how they went to see *Gone with the Wind*. It was a nice, pleasant evening that February in 1940. And then, ironically, a strong wind blew up, carrying the strong aroma of McEwan's export in its wake. Just one sniff and Harry was gone. Not to the chippie, in Orr Street, but to the inviting pub across the way in Dalmarnock Road. But Aggie forgave him for, being the gentleman he was, he returned carrying the mandatory fish and sixpence of chips.

Alas, that palace of dreams was now no more. That tiled citadel had, at one point, succumbed to the greedy appetite of the dragon called *bingo*. And then, as that beast's fire was extinguished, it became a storage warehouse for furniture.

But even that was now gone. The building was redundant, ignominiously discarded and no longer even wanted for storing furniture. But it still stored the dreams and wishes of past young couples, sweethearts who sat in the back row embracing and dreaming. Aggie smiled as the memories of Bridgeton Cross and the Olympia filled her mind. She turned and walked towards the umbrella. A slight drizzle had come on and Aggie hurried on into the shelter.

One toothless old man, sitting on a bench and puffing on a yellowing clay pipe looked up.

'Aye, ye'd better get under, hen,' he said. 'It could come doon hard.'

'Aye, ye're right,' Aggie agreed.

The old man shoved the scruffy individual, who sat next to him, along a bit and gestured, with a nod, to Aggie to occupy the now vacant space. Aggie thanked him and sat down.

'Thanks a lot,' she said, 'dae ye . . . er sit here o'ften?'

'Only when Ah'm eatin' mince,' the old bloke said.

'Where's the mince, then?' Aggie asked.

'Ah've ate it.' The man said, drawing the back of his hand across his mouth.

'Who gave ye the mince?' Aggie was intrigued.

'Ah don't know his name but he comes up here on a butcher's bike and gies us it,' he said.

'He's a good Samaratin, eh?' Aggie said.

'Aye, Ah think that's his name,' the man said.

'Whit's his name?' Aggie asked.

'Sam Martin,' the old bloke said.

Aggie sighed and smiled to herself. 'And whit's your name?' she asked, always wanting to know to whom she was talking.

'Jones,' the man said, taking a puff at his pipe and throwing a spit five yards.

'Hiv ye got a first name?' Aggie asked.

The man nodded, 'Aye, of coorse,' he said, 'it's Indiana.'

Aggie raised her eyebrows, 'Oh, aye,' she said, 'yer maw gie ye that name?'

The old man nodded. 'Aye, she called a' her weans efter places.'

'Ah would think that Indiana Jones wisnae known when you wur born,' Aggie said.

'Ma maw was a spey wife,' the man said. 'She could look in tae the future.'

'And she saw Indiana Jones before Hollywood did, that it?' Aggie said with scepticism.

'Right,' the wee man said. 'She liked the name so she called me Indiana!'

'Interestin,' Aggie said.

'Ah'm jist gled Ah wisnae ma brother, Anniesland,' the old man said, screwing up his nose.

'Anniesland Jones, eh?' Aggie laughed.

'We called him Annie for short,' the wee man said.

'That figgers,' Aggie said. Her eyes went to the scruffy individual who had been shoved along the bench by Indiana's backside. What a pitiful sight, Aggie thought. Scraggly, matted beard, a greasy, shining overcoat and, if she thought Indiana's pipe was yellow, this poor soul's teeth was the colour of ripened bananas. She sadly shook her head. Some people get dealt a duff haun, she thought.

'So, ye say yer maw was a speywife?' she said.

Indiana nodded. 'Aye, she was uncanny,' he said proudly. 'She predicted that ma faither would die violently.'

'And did he?' Aggie asked frowning.

'Aye, he did,' the wee man said. 'He came in late wan night and she hit him wi' the hatchet.'

'And whit happened tae yer maw?' Aggie asked, curiously.

'It was in a' the papers,' Indiana said, spreading his hands out. 'Big headlines – *Big Fat Manky Molly Sentenced for Murder* – Oh, she was executed,' Indiana said, spitting a full eight yards.

'Whit a shame!' Aggie said. 'They didnae have tae say she was fat and manky,' she added.

'But she was,' the wee man said, removing his pipe from his

mouth to emphasise the point. 'She was forty-two stones,' he added.

'Big wumman, right enough,' Aggie agreed, 'and manky as well, eh?' she added.

'They gave her a bath before they took her tae the execution chamber,' the wee man said. 'A good scrub. When she stepped oot that bath she was jist eight-stone two.'

'Then they gave her the chair, that it?' Aggie said.

'Naw, the bed,' Indiana said. 'They gave her a lethal injection.

'Whit did they inject her wee boady wi' – strychnine?' Aggie shuddered.

'Domestos,' he replied.

'And that was you left wi' yer brother, Annie, right?' Aggie said.

The wee man nodded. 'Aye, we wur orphans efter that. Ma da' gone wi' a hatchet in his heid and ma maw scrubbed – mind ye, ma da' always said she was a scrubber,' he shook his head sadly.

'Aye, we've a' got troubles, son,' Aggie murmured, thinking of her own problems. She nodded towards 'banana teeth'.

'That yer brother?' she asked.

'Who?" Old Jones asked.

'There,' Aggie said, indicating with a jab of her thumb, 'banana teeth.'

'Naw, naw,' the wee man said. 'that's ma wife.'

'*Yer wife!*' Aggie cried. She just could not believe that this scruffy, bearded, pitiful person with the coat that looked like it had been painted with lard was a human being never mind a woman.

'Her wi' the yella teeth is your wife?' she said shocked.

'They're false,' the wee man said.

'Her chist or her teeth?' Aggie asked.

'Her teeth,' was the reply.

'Ye mean she got *yella* false teeth?'

'She wanted them for tae look like her real teeth when she had them,' he said, removing his pipe and wiping his mouth.

'So, whit happened tae her real teeth?' Aggie said.

'She blamed a' they adverts for toothpaste in the demise of her teeth,' he answered. 'She thought that the modern toothpaste was too strong wi' every other brand gettin' stronger and stronger. The adverts wur showin' how good and tasty and strong their tooth-paste was. Ye wur gettin' it shoved doon yer throat.'

'So, whit's that got tae dae wi' anythin'?' Aggie said.

'Well, she got the very latest toothpaste, hopin' for to replace her yella teeth wi' gleamin white teeth. *You'll wonder where the yella' went* it said on the tube and she couldnae wait tae try it. It took jist wan brushin'.'

'And did she wonder where the yella went?' Aggie asked, raising her brows.

'She wondered where her teeth went,' the wee man said.

Aggie began to wonder about Mr Jones. 'Whit's yer wife's name Mr Jones?' she asked.

'Catherine Zeta,' Indiana replied.

'Catherine Zeta Jones?' Aggie cried.

'It's no' her real name,' the wee man said. 'She chinged it by Deed Poll.'

'Ah didnae think it would be,' Aggie replied, adding, 'Whit *is* her real name?'

' Gladys Zeta Jones,' Indiana replied.

'Ur you sure she's a wumman?' Aggie said, narrowing her eyes.

'Oh, she's a wumman a'right. Ah can vouch for that. Whit makes ye doubt it?' he replied, puzzled.

'Well, the beard for a start,' Aggie said.

'Ach don't let that fool ye,' the man said, 'I made her wear that – it's false, ye know – cos Ah'm a very jealous man.'

'Jealous?' Aggie gasped.

'She attracts men like flies followin' diarrhoeac elephants. They jist canny keep their haun's oaff her. Men of a' stations in life. Ah'v seen her walkin' intae the posh Hilton Hotel wearin' nothin' special, jist like she's dressed noo and bein' thrown oot the door 'cos they knew there would be a stampede o' droolin' men wance they got a glimpse o' her. Ah've tae keep an eye on her a' the bloody time.'

Gladys was delighted by her husband's obvious jealousy. She squeezed his hand and gave Aggie a flashing yellow smile.

'Ah jist canny help it, so Ah canny,' she said. 'Wan flash o' ma teeth and they want tae take me oot.'

'Ur ye sure it's no' yer teeth they want tae take oot?' Aggie said.

'Ah could've been a model,' Gladys said, showing her bananas to great advantage.

'She *did* model wance,' Indiana said proudly. 'Tell her aboot it, Sugerplum,' he said, pecking Gladys' cheek.

Gladys sighed. 'Aw, aye, we wur doon in Millport at the time – remember hootchy-coo – the famous hoat peas?'

'Aye, Ah had a uninery infection at the time,' her husband said, grimacing.

'Well,' Gladys went on, 'this very artistic man came up tae me and asked if Ah would model for a sculpture he was daein.'

'Wur you flattered?' Aggie said.

'Naw, Ah was staunin' up at the time,' Gladys said. 'Anywey, he got a big lump o' rock and got tae work on me.'

'Ah'd like tae get tae work on ye wi' a big lump o' rock,' Indy said.

'He said Ah'd be immortal,' Gladys said with an even wider grin.

'An' so she is, ma wee Millport petal,' Indiana said.

'An' did he finish the sculpture that was tae make her immortal?' Aggie asked.

'He did – and it's there to this day. A monument tae ma Gladys for to be gazed on lovingly for ever and ever.'

'Ah canny say that Ah remember anythin' like that doon in Millport,' Aggie said, racking her brains.

'*Whit?*' Indy cried, ' Don't tell me ye hiv never seeen Millport's famous Crocodile Rock?'

Aggie laughed. 'So,' she said, changing the subject, 'ye've had yer mince,eh?'

The wee man nodded.

'Whit aboot a vindaloo, noo?' Aggie said.

'Naw, the mince hisnae taken affect yet,' the wee man said. 'Besides, the lavvies are a' blocked aff noo.'

'Ah meant a nice plate o' hoat curry,' Aggie said.

She kept going back to the Bible story. The man organised a feast, gave out the invitations and got nothing but excuses from the invited guests. So, he ordered his servants to go out into the streets and bring in the poor and the crippled and anybody else that would come. Indiana Jones and his wife, Catherine Zeta, looked like they stepped right out of the Good Book's pages. Catherine, now Gladys, wore a fox fur that Aggie looked on with deep suspicion. Not only was it foaming at the mouth but she didn't like the agresssive look in its eye or the way its leg was cocked and ready for action. Still, she cleared her throat and, once more, invited them up to the house to help celebrate.

'Aw, come on,' she said, half pleading, 'ye'll enjoy yersels, so ye will,' she said.

The wee man in the greasy coat licked his palm and held it out, 'Right hen, ye've got a deal', he said, pumping her hand.

Aggie smiled and rubbed her hand up and down her thigh. 'You tae,' she said to Mrs Jones who stood up and kissed her.

Aggie grimaced but inside felt that she had at last broken the jinx. Indiana and Gladys Zeta Jones, Nancy and herself was an improvement. She felt quite happy as they left the Umbrella and crossed busy Bridgeton Cross towards London Road.

It was still early enough for guests to arrive and Aggie consoled herself with that thought. But where oh where was Nancy? Her mind ran through a catalogue of nasty things that may have happened to her daughter. She thought, too, of Wee Alice but then dismissed the idea as preposterous. Nobody, but nobody would attack Alice. She *had* been attractive before her Charles Bronson days. But anybody accosting her would immediately associate her with *Death Wish* and take off pronto.

As they walked along Aggie felt suddenly elated. She looked towards the heavens and whispered, 'Thanks Harry for no' makin' me celebrate oor anniversary by masel'.'

She put an arm around Indiana's shoulder and gave him an affectionate squeeze. But she pulled her arm away quickly as she felt something crawling up her sleeve. It was a mouse. Aggie let out a yell and the wee man laughed.

'Sorry aboot that,' he said. 'Ah don't know where they come frae but they seem tae target me for some reason. Dae ye think Ah should get a bath?'

'Ah think ye should get a cat,' Aggie said.

'Aye, right enough,' the man said.

Aggie shuddered and wondered if it was taking a bit of a risk bringing Hansel and Gretel into her spick-and-span home? But she soon shrugged that notion off. Harry had sent her guests to enjoy this special day with her. And Aggie was glad, yes, Aggie *was* glad. They walked on. If only she would hear from Nancy who, she had decided, was lying somewhere with a hatchet in her skull.

Aggie did not hear the scream of the car's tyres as it swung alongside the trio. Two burly policemen got out.

'Right, *you*!' The taller one snapped, 'Staun' where ye ur — at *wance*!'

Aggie was startled and her jaw dropped.

'Right, Wullie,' the big cop growled, 'cuff them.'

The smaller policeman shrugged and immediately cuffed the three of them on the ears.

'Naw, naw,' the big cop said with impatience, '*Cuff them* – that means put the handcuffs oan them no' hit them oan the face.'

'Aw, sorry,' the wee cop said and proceeded to carry out his order.

'He's new,' the big man said in way of mitigation.

'Whit's this a' aboot?' Aggie snapped.

'Youse were a' seen shopliftin' in *Marks an' Spencers* in Sauchiehall Street earlier oan.'

'No' us,' Aggie protested.

'Aye youse,' the big cop stated. 'We've only got a description of two o' ye, you two.' He pointed to the manky couple.

'Whit description is that, then?' Indiana snapped.

'Two greasy men wi' shiney overcoats and manky hair,' the policeman said.

'Ah, wel youse ur wrang there, see,' Gladys cried loudly. 'We ur not *two* greasy men, see. We ur *wan* greasy man and Ah am a greasy wumman, so there. Ah take the Fifth Amendment.'

'You ur in the wrang country for that,' the policeman said. 'Ah am not Kojak and we don't hiv any fifth amendments – no' even wan, two three and four wans – so there.'

Aggie and her new friends were bundled into the police car which speeded off, sirens wailing.

The desk sergeant at the London Road Police Station peered over the top his glasses as they were led inside protesting vehemently.

'The shop lifters frae Marks an' Spencers,' the big man said, leading them to face the stern face of the man in charge.

'Right,' the sergeant said, licking his pencil and looking at Indiana.

'Name?' he snapped.

'Tom Cruise,' the wee man replied.

'Oh, aye, a funny man, eh?' the sergeant said, his eyes narrowing. He nodded towards Gladys.

'Ah suppose this is Nicole Kidman?' he said.

'Don't be daft,' Gladys blurted, 'dae Ah look like Nicole Kidman?'

'A'right, then,' the sergeant said, 'whit *is* yer name?'

'Julia Roberts,' Gladys said.

The sergeant raised his eyes to heaven in despair. 'An' you, whit aboot you?' he said to Aggie.

'Betty Grable,' Aggie said, capitulating to the whole scene.

Turning to the arresting officers, the sergeant said, 'Whit did they pinch?'

'It wisnae soap anyway,' the big cop said.

'Hiv ye searched them?' the sergeant asked.

'Jist him,' the cop said.

'Whit did ye find, then?' the sergeant said.

'A' a found was a deid moose – in his heid.'

'Better get them two fumigated,' the sergeant said, 'and loack this wan up in the cell.'

Aggie protested her innocence. 'Ah don't even know this couple,' she cried.

'Nae excuse,' the sergeant said.'Right,' he went on pointing to the couple, 'youse go alang wi' constable Clint Eastwood, there, for to be fumigated and you,' he said to Aggie, 'go wi' DI Frost for to be loacked up while inquiries continue.'

DI Frost took Aggie by the arm and she was about to be led away when the constable who arrested Sammy happened to walk in.

'Whit's this?' he said, in surprise.

'This wumman and a smelly couple wur picked up for shopliftin' in Sauchiehall Street earlier,' the sergeant said.

'How earlier?' asked the cop, whose granny was a mere ninety-two.

99

'Aboot three hoors ago,' the sergeant said.

'Impossible!' Constable ninety-two said. 'Ah was in her hoose then arrestin' her brother,Sammy.'

'Ye mean wee singin' Sammy? Him that kept singin' *The Blue, Blue Grass Of Home*? in there?' the sergeant said.

'Aye, well he's a Rangers supporter,' the policeman said.

'So you reckon she couldnae hiv been with the scruffy couple there, eh?'

'Impossible,' the cop said.

'Right, then,' the sergeant said 'away you go hame, hen.'

Aggie sighed and thanked policeman ninety-two for saving her bacon. Turning to the sergeant, she said. 'Hiv some pity on they two. They live in a dream world, so they dae. He thinks he's Indiana Jones and has got her brainwashed as well.'

'That's aboot the only part o' her that's washed, then,' the sergeant said.

It suddenly struck Aggie that she was in the right place to seek help. 'While Ah'm here,' she said, 'Ah'd like for to report ma daughter missin'.'

'Oh?' the sergeant's eyebrows went up. 'How long has she been missin'?' he said.

'Aboot two hoors,' Aggie said.

'Oh, aye,' the sergeant said, putting his pencil down on the desk. 'And how auld is she?'

'Twinty-nine,' Ah think,' Aggie said, racking her brains.

'Well, Ah say the chances are that she's oot wi' her boyfriend hivin' a good time,' the policeman said, 'Ah, mean, two oors? Hive ye checked the lavvy? Ma wife vanishes for two oors and that's usually where she's been.'

'Nancy is not in the lavvy, Ah can assure you of that,' Aggie said angrily.

'Ah'll mark doon that you hiv made a report o' yer auld lassie missin' but that's aboot a' Ah can dae at this stage,' he said, picking up his pencil and licking it.

Aggie left the police station devasted. She looked up to heaven and, stopping herself from shaking her fist, said. 'Right, Harry, whit's the gemme? Ah'm right back where Ah started – even worse, in fact. Never mind they two being whisked away frae me, everybody else is away an' a' – even oor Nancy. Ah'll jist keep tryin'. Ah do *nut* want tae celebrate oor golden day by masel', so Ah don't. It's no' fair, so it's no.' Aggie dabbed her eye but, instead of heading for home, turned, crossed the road and headed down James' Street towards the Glasgow Green where she was sure she could solve her problem.

She licked the tip of her finger and made an invisible tick in the air. Gladys and her husband were undoubtedly poor and, although they had been unable to accept her invitation, due to arresting circumstances, she had, at least, tried. One consolation was that the unfortunate pair would have a hearty meal and a warm bed for the night. That pleased Aggie.

Passing a shop doorway she heard the rattle of a tin and a voice saying. 'Hey missus, you wi' the checked coat, spare a copper for a poor blind man.'

Aggie turned. In the doorway a beggar sat rattling a tin mug and at his feet, head between outstretched paws, a shaggy mongrel dog .

'Did you speak tae me?' Aggie said.

'Who – who is that, talkin' tae a poor blind man?' the man said.

'It's me, the wumman wi' the checked coat – and you're a fraud, so ye ur. How could ye tell Ah'm wearin' a checked coat if ye canny see, eh?'

'Ah hivnae said a word, missus, so Ah hivnae,' the beggar said.

'Ah distinctly heard ye ask for money as Ah passed by,' Aggie said.

'No' me, missus – it was the dug – it's a ventriloquist.'

'Ye must think ma heid buttons up the back,' Aggie snapped.

'Ah'm jist a poor blind man tryin' for tae eke oot a livin', so Ah am.'

'Aye, well, ye're definitely at it,' Aggie said. 'You ur nut blind, so you're no' and Ah'll prove it.' Aggie held up her hand. 'How many fingers am Ah haudin' up?' she said sharply.

'Twelve,' the beggar said.

'How can Ah hiv twelve fingers?' Aggie snapped.

'The dug whispered tae me,' the man said.

'Well, yer dug needs glesses,'Aggie said.

'Don't you say anythin'aboot ma dug.'The man was cross. 'Jist because he's nae good at countin'. Ah would be loast without ma wee pal. That is a very talented dug, so it is. Even its fleas ur trained.'

'Trained?' Aggie's brows shot up. 'He's only a wee mongrel.'

'He might be a wee mongrel tae you hen, but his fleas are pedigreed.'

Aggie tried to hide a smile. 'Pedigreed?' she repeated.

'They're that regal he's got tae ask permission before he'll scratch,' the beggar said.

'Aye, right,' Aggie said, not believing one word of it. 'Whit's yer dug's name?'

'Rory,' the beggar said. 'that's ma wee Rory.'

'A good name for a dug,' Aggie said. 'Whit made ye pick that name?'

'He's a great impersonator,' the beggar said.

'Jist like his maister who's impersonatin' a blind man,eh?'

'You can think whit ye like, hen,' he said. 'But ye canny take anythin' away frae ma dug. The greatest animal impersonator in Hollywood.'

'Oh, so yer dug's a film star, is he?' Aggie sneered.

'Did ye ever see *Lassie Come Home?*' the man asked.

'Don't tell me yer dug was in that?' Aggie said.

'He *wis* Lassie,' he said proudly.

'Ach, away ye go,' Aggie scoffed. 'Lassie was ma sister Dolly, no' a shaggy-lookin' wee mongrel like him.'

The dog growled and Aggie stepped back a pace.

'Ah'm tellin' ye, he's the greatest impersonator in the world,' the man said, 'every picture ye've ever seen starrin' an animal it was him.' He nodded towards the pooch.

'*Every* picture?' Aggie said, her tongue in her cheek.

'Did ye ever see *King Kong?*' the man said nodding towards the dog.

'Ye don't tell me?' Aggie said.

'See that lion that opens every MGM picture?'

'Ye don't say!' Aggie said.

'It's no' a lion at a' – its him,' nodding towards the dog again.

'Wonderful!' Aggie said. 'He'll be puttin' Rory Bremner oot o' business. Can he dae anything'?'

'Anythin',' the man replied. 'You should see him daein' Elvis.'

'Naw, naw, spare me that, 'Aggie said, grimacing. 'Anywey, that's no' the reason Ah'm doon here.'

'Whit's up, hen?' the beggar said, 'Ah can hear somethin' in yer voice.'

'Whit can ye hear?' Aggie said.

'Yer teeth rattlin',' the man said.

'It's yer tin cup ye hear rattlin',' Aggie said.

'Say nuthin' aboot that cup,' the man in the doorway said.

'Don't tell me it's the Holy Grail,' Aggie said, her hand coming up to her mouth.

'That cup is a replica of the great 1966 World Cup won by England and whit we are never gonny be allowed tae forget.'

'That was never a World Cup,' Aggie said.

'The real World Cup was melted doon an' made in tae mugs for fanatical supporters south of the border, and selt at ninety quid a time. They selt thousands o' them for tae get money tae help build a new stadium at Wembley.' The man said.

'They must've had a loat o' supporters,' Aggie said.

'They had a loat o' mugs,' the beggar said.

Aggie was beginning to think that this blind man was takin' a len' o' her' and was about to call his bluff when she heard a commotion.

A bunch of girls were coming along the pavement, shouting and laughing and generally making merriment. At the centre of the group was an embarrassed girl decked out in gaily coloured crepe paper bunting, with a chamberpot on her head and carrying another, filled with salt and confetti. The girls were dancing and singing around the bride, for that's what she was, and the high-spirited chorus sang loudly the saga of Frankie and Johnny.

Aggie smiled. She thought that this tradition had died out years ago. It was once a common sight to see a blushing bride being paraded through the streets, decked out like a Christmas tree, by her happy-go-lucky pals. Her chanty full of salt was supposed to bring good luck and prosperity. Usually the ritual was instigated by her colleagues from the factory where she worked. It was a show of affection and a genuine wish that the girl

103

would find a happy life with her man. This was a send-off into the sea of matrimony, a bon-voyage to happiness. This was the boat being pushed out – the Love Boat.

Aggie was pleased the happy tradition was still alive. She remembered her own launching by her friends at Templetons carpet factory where she worked. Of how they pounced on her the minute the factory whistle blew. Decked her out, paraded her up Arcadia Street and down London Road. Of how some drunks, even at this comparatively early evening hour, staggered up and, pumping her hand, gave her the traditional warm Glasgow greeting of, 'A' Ra Best, Hen, A' ra best!'

Alas, no Templetons carpets were produced there now and only the majestic palace that would not have been out of place in an Arabian desert stood as a monument to a bygone age when they produced the finest carpets that graced the finest homes.

Aggie pecked the new bride on the cheek. 'A' ra best, hen,' she said, affectionately.

'Thanks missus,' the girl said.

'You haud oan tae yer man, hen, haud oan tae him,' Aggie said, patting the girls's cheek.

'Did you haud oantae yours, missus?' the girl said with a wry smile.

'Every Setturday night, hen,' Aggie laughed. 'Ah had tae or he would've fell doon the stairs.'

The girl laughed and was dragged on by her entourage to the loud chanting of *Please Release Me.*

The man with the dog heard all this and felt Aggie's distress. 'Ah . . . er . . . Ah feel ye sound a wee bit distressed, missus,' the doggie man said. 'Ur ye a'right?'

Aggie sighed. 'This is ma golden weddin' anniversary,' she said. 'Fifty years when Ah walked doon the aisle tae the waitin' erms o' ma Harry.'

'So, whit's yer problem, missus?' the beggar asked.

'Ma Harry is no longer wi' me.' Aggie said quietly.

'Away wi' younger wumman, is he?'

Aggie shook her head. 'Naw, naw, he's deid,' she said quickly.

'And ye're still haudin' yer anniversary?' the man said with disbelief.

'We made a proamise tae each other that no matter whit, we'd haud oor anniversary,' Aggie said.

'A'right, then,' the man said, 'so ye're keepin' yer word – whit's the trouble?'

'Naebody has replied tae ma invitation and naebody has turned up tae celebrate wi' me. And, so Ah'm takin' a leaf oot the Good Book and here Ah am intae the streets tae seek oot the blind and the poor and the crippled and like the ma in the Bible did, invite them tae help me celebrate.'

'Luke, Chapter 14, verses 15 to 24,' the beggar said.

'Ye know yer Bible, eh?' Aggie said.

'Ma maw rammed it doon ma throat when Ah was a boy,' he said. 'In fact the weans at school used tae call me Elijah.' The beggar grimced. 'Ah mean, who would want a name like Elijah McGeachie, eh?'

'Whit *is* yer first name?' Aggie asked.

'Pontius,' he said.

'Well, Pontius,' Aggie said, 'Ah feel Harry and me hiv been let down by oor so-called freens. But Ah'm no' gonny let them get me down. Wull you come hame wi' me for ma celebration?'

'The dug an' a'?' he asked.

'He can entertain us,' Aggie said.

'Right,' the man said, rising to his feet, 'If ye want mair o' us white stick brigade, why no' invite some o' the cataract chabanc crowd alang. They'll fill yer hoose.'

'The cataract charabanc crowd?' Aggie enquired.

'They're frae China and are here on a tour o' Scotland.' The beggar said. 'They're goin' tae Rothesay the morra and they're takin' me wi' them.'

'Aw. That's nice,' Aggie said. 'Where are they the noo?'

'They're roon' at the mission hall doon the green. C'mon. Ah'll take ye doon and ye can ask them alang yersel,' the beggar said, tugging at the sleeping dog, who growled and got to its feet.

'There's only aboot a dozen o' the charabanc crowd,' the beggar adding 'so they'll no' eat ye oot a hoose an' hame.'

'That disnae matter,' Aggie said. 'It'll please me and Harry.'

The trio made their way down towards Glasgow Green and the mission hall. They could hear the raucous singing of *We Shall*

Gather at the River as they turned into Greenhead Street.

A short, tubby man conducted the singing from a dais at the end of the room. When the last note faded, he rapped a stick on top of the table and called for order.

'That was worthy of the Mormon Tabernacle Choir,' he said. 'It won't be the river we'll be gathering at in the morning, but the Wemyss Bay Ferry Terminal.'

A loud burst of applause greeted this announcement.

'Jist a minute Mr Graham,' Pontius called out.

'Aye, Pontius, whit is it?' the roly-poly man replied.

'There's a wumman here celebratin' her golden weddin' anniversary and wants us a' for tae come alang tae her hoose and help her celebrate.'

A round of applause greeted the announcement. One Chinese tourist stood up.

'That is very kind of you . . . er . . . Mrs . . . er . . . ?' the wee fat man said.

'Gallagher,' Aggie replied.

'Mrs Gallagher,' he repeated.

The hall echoed with loud, excited Chinese chatter and Mr Graham had to rap his stick once more on the table top.

'Friends,' he called out, but his cry was unheeded and he had to, once more, batter his stick off the table. 'Friends,' he cried, '*Chinas!*,' he yelled, using the well known Glasgow patois for a friend or sometimes a boozing pal. The babble died down.

'It's well known that Glasgow hospitality is the best in the world and we must thank Mrs Gallagher . . .'

'Aggie,' Aggie interrupted.

'Er . . . Aggie,' Mr Graham continued, 'We must thank Aggie for her kind invitation. Ah know youse appreciate it and it will gie – give youse a chance for to enjoy some real Scottish cooking.'

Another loud burst of applause.

'And whit will you be treatin' oor Chinese visitors to, Mrs Gallagher? Whit feast will they return hame praisin' oor good auld fashioned Scottish culinary delights?'

'Vindaloos,' Aggie said.

The word was uttered around the hall by the quizzical Chinese tourists.

'Ah – vindaloo?'

'A good auld fashioned Scottish dish,' Aggie said. 'It's gaelic for yer faither's mince in the pan.'

'Ah, minch in honourable pan – mm!'

'Aye,' Aggie assured them, '*Vin* means mince *Da* means yer faither and *Loo* means pan. It was a great delicacy wi' Robert the Bruce's men, so it was.'

'Robert the Bruce was a great Scottish warrior,' the wee fat man interrupted.

'Ah, Wallior,' grew the mumble approvingly.

'Aye, jist before a battle his men would mount their hoarses, pull oot their dirks and gallop forward screamin' *Vindaloo!*'

'Pull oot honourable dilcks – loverly,' the lady tourists blushed.

'Ret's go.' Up went the cry.

Mr Graham ushered the group out of the hall and on to the waiting bus. The men, arms raised and with clenched fists cried out with gusto – *Vindargo!*

Aggie clambered aboard her heart bursting with happiness. She glanced skywards.

'Thanks, Harry,' she said, dabbing her eye. 'Noo we can hiv a real celebration!'

Aggie always looked up to heaven when she talked to Harry although sometimes she did look down a stank. She had rounded up the blind and had almost captured the poor, and although Indiana and his bearded wife didn't quite make it, she was glad to see that they would have a warm place to lay their heads this night and be satisfied with a hearty meal.

Chinese chatter filled the bus and Aggie was delighted. She thought of Dolly and Sammy and Chu Chu who could not or would not stay with her – and wee Alice. What had happened to her? And where was Nancy? Well, the police knew about Nancy and there was nothing she could do – except worry. Her daughter would want her to go ahead with the planned celebrations no matter what. Aggie looked around the bus and listened to the happy chatter. Yes, everything was working out fine. That man in the Bible had good ideas.

The bus driver was the last to board and take his seat behind the wheel. He turned and gave Aggie a quizzical look. Aggie cleared her throat and gave him directions and seconds later the engine burst into life. They were on their way. The big party was about to begin.

At first nobody heard the wee fat man's mobile phone ring. 'Hello,' he said, pressing the phone against his right ear. But even at that the engine noise and the loud chatter made it difficult for him to catch what the caller was saying.

He held up his hand. 'Quiet, please,' he cried. There was no response. '*Quiet!*' he bawled.

Still no response. The visitors were too caught up in their happy conversations.

'*Shut yer geggies!*' Aggie hollered. And as though somebody had switched off the volume control, there was a sudden silence. Only Mr Graham's voice could be heard.

'Yes,' he was saying. 'Are ye sure? Aw, whit a shame! Is that definite . . . aye, right.'

Aggie didn't like the sound of this. The wee man folded the phone and slipped it into his inside jacket pocket.

'Stoap the bus,' he ordered.

The driver stood on the brakes and the bus screeched to a halt.

'Friends,' the wee fat man began, 'Ah'm sorry but we must forgo the kind invitation by Mrs Ga . . . er . . . Aggie.'

Aggie's heart slumped as she listened.

An interpretor translated and there was a sad sigh from the visitors.

'The ferrymen are goin' on strike the morra which means we would nut be able for tae go ower tae the lovely Isle of Bute and feast oor eyes on the marvellous Victorian lavvies. Many famous people have used them lavvies and Ah'm sorry that youse wull not have the opportunity for to christen them.'

The interpretor finished and a disappointed hush enveloped the bus.

'Nae vindaloo?' cried one of the more educated visitors.

'Nae Victorian Loo,' Mr Graham said. 'But,' he went on, 'There is wan chance we could make it ower tae Rothesay. If we can get doon tae Wemyss Bay within the next three oors, we could catch a ferry before the strike starts Ah've been assured. So, sorry Mrs Gal . . . er . . . Aggie.'

108

The wee man sounded genuinely sorry.

Aggie shrugged. She tried to look as nonchalant as possible. But inside she was being torn apart.

'It canny be helped,' she found herself saying. 'Ah'm sure youse wull enjoy Rothesay. Staunin' there watchin' the steamers an' that.'

'Velly solly Mrs Garragher,' a little man said. 'Maybe some other time get Mr Bluce's vinderoo.'

Aggie turned to Pontius. 'You go and enjoy yersel', son,' she said, 'Ah'm jist a bit disappointed. Ah was hopin' yer dug would've gied us a quick chorus of *My Way*.'

The beggar smiled. 'He disnae know that yin,' he said, 'but he could've gied ye a good rendition of Tchiacovsky's Piano Concerto on yer old Joanna.'

Aggie laughed and stepped off the bus to a chorus of 'Cheelios'.

She stood on the pavement and watched the bus pull away with a raucous chorus of *Prease lelease me Ret me Go* ringing in her ears.

A slight drizzle had come on as she watched the red tail lights of the bus go to the top of James Street and vanish round the corner into Bridgeton Cross. She turned up the collar of her coat, stood still for a moment and took her bearings.

Where to now, she wondered?

CHAPTER FOUR

THE RAIN GREW HEAVIER AS AGGIE TURNED INTO DALMARNOCK Road. She cursed herself for not bringing an umbrella with her and tightened her coat around her neck. Ahead, she saw the parish church where she and Harry had wed that whole lifetime ago and wondered if the Reverend Mr McGinty was still alive? Why shouldn't he be, she thought? This was his first parish and he was a comparatively young man at the time.

Aggie hurried on and found herself tugging at the large, brass doorbell of the manse. The door finally creaked open and the little minister stood before her. The Reverend McGinty had changed since their last encounter. Gone was the tall, slim, youthful man now replaced by a slightly bent, balding gentleman who was now peering over the top of his gold-rimmed pinz-nez.

'Yes?' he croaked in a shallow, squeaky voice .

'Er . . . Mr McGinty is that you?' Aggie stammered.

'Ah gave tae you last week,' the voice said.

'Naw, naw, Mr McGinty,' Aggie said quickly, 'Ah'm no' collectin' for anythin'.'

Mr McGinty narrowed his eyes, 'You're no' frae the RRBS?'

'Ah don't even know whit the RRBS is,' Aggie said.

'It's the Royal Redundant Butlers Society,' Mr McGinty said.

'Naw, no' me,' Aggie said.

'Well, ye'd better come in, then,' the minister said. Opening the door wide he ushered Aggie into a large well furnished room that smelled of furniture polish. He indicated a large easy chair which Aggie sank into. Mr McGinty sat on a similar chair facing her. Placing his hands together Steeple fashion, he leaned back.

'Right, hen,' he said, 'whit can Ah dae for ye?'

'Dae ye no' recognise me?' Aggie said, fluttering her eyelashes.

'Ah don't know anybody wi' an eye affliction like that,' he said.

'You married me,' Aggie said.

The minister shot bolt upright.

'Ah did *nut*!' he snapped. 'Ah am married tae ma Ethel and hiv been for twenty-two years. Ah know for a fact that you ur nae her. Besides she hisnae got flutterin' keekers.'

'Naw, naw, Ah don't mean we ur married tae each other,' Aggie said. 'You ur the minister that officiated at ma weddin' fifty years ago. This is ma golden weddin' anniversary,' Aggie blurted. 'Dae ye no' recognise me?'

The minister peered over the top of his glasses. 'Mmm!' he murmered. 'Yer coupon does hiv some familiarity aboot it. But that disnae mean anythin'. Ah keep mixin' up faces. Ah sometimes mix up ma Ethel's face wi' Bunty's.'

'Who's Bunty?' Aggie asked.

'The dug,' Mr McGinty said.

'It was fifty years ago that you joined me and ma Harry together in holy matrimony,' Aggie said dreamily. 'Dae ye no remember? Ma da' gave me away.'

'How, whit had ye done?' the minister asked suspiciously.

'Ma da' escorted me doon the aisle as faither's dae,' Aggie said. 'He was a sailor – mind?'

Mr McGinty screwed up his eyes. He was thinking deeply. He peered into Aggie's face, their noses almost touching. Suddenly he snapped his fingers.

'Yer da' bein' a sailor brings it a' back tae me,' he cried. 'Ah remember sayin' it was the first time Ah'd seen a sailor gien' his daughter away . . . aye, Ah mind fine.' Mr McGinty sounded pleased with himself.

'Ye don't get many sailors walkin' doon yer aisle, then?' Aggie said.

'No' Admirals o' the Fleet ye don't,' the minister replied.

'Aye ma da' was a very strikin' man,' Aggie said.

'A good union man, eh?'

'Naw, Ah mean he stood oot in a crowd,' Aggie said.

'Aye, right enough,' Mr McGinty said, 'he was seven-feet-two tall, wint he?'

'Naw, ma da' was only five-fit four, but he had chronic veruccas.'

'Aye, well we've a' got oor shortcomings,' the minister said. 'But he was every bit a matlow for a' that. Ah remember how striking youse were walkin' doon that aisle. It was like lookin' at that bloke oan the Players cigarette packet – the full set – a healthy beard and moustache – long before Captain Birdseye's day.'

'Aye, Ah remember it well masel.' Aggie sighed.

'Yer faither looked good as well,' the minister said.

'Yer man, Hairy, wint it?' he went on.

'Harry,' Aggie corrected.

'Aye, the general. He arrived an oor before you – aw nervous. Soon as Ah saw him he reminded me of India for some reason.'

'How was that?' Aggie asked.

'He was eatin' a curry cairry-oot while he waited for you,' the minister said, adding a loud, yuech!

'Eatin' a curry?' Aggie couldn't believe it.

'Wi' his fingers,' the minister said, grimacing.

'He must've been hungry,' Aggie said by way of an apology.

'It was the maist unusual weddin' Ah hiv ever officiated at,' the minister went on.

'In whit wey?' Aggie asked.

'Yer wee flower girl for instance,' Mr McGinty, said, with a quick glance towards heaven, 'she was at least eighty-two – a funny lookin' individual.'

'Ah know, Ah know,' Aggie said. 'you thought it was ma gran'-mother, that it?'

'Ah thought it was yer gran' *faither*,' the minister said adding, 'an' another thing that made it unusual was yer mode of trans-port.'

'Aye, well, Harry, bein' a cavalry man, thought we'd dispense wi' the usual bridal car and hiv a different kinda bridle and that was the reason we had two hoarses – very romantic so it was,' Aggie sighed.

'Romantic, maybe,' the minister said, 'but Ah don't usually allow hoarses in the church.'

'Aye, well, Harry appreciated it, so he did,' Aggie said. 'He even gave his best man a brush in case of accidents. Very thoughtful that wey, was Harry.'

'That's another thing,' Mr McGinty said, 'that best man, he stood there for a whole oor and never wance removed his helmet, Sheer bad manners.'

'A lot o' servicemen hiv tae keep their helmets on,' Aggie said, 'because it's military regulations. They'd be done for bein' oot o' uniform.'

'It was a weddin' and he should've made an exception,' the minister said. 'Deep Sea divers should be in a special category!'

Aggie agreed. Harry's best man had found it hard to hear what was going on and the minister had to bang him on the head now and again with a brass candlestick.

'Ah remember yer mother being pushed up the aisle just in time for the ceremony.' Mr McGinty said.

'Ma maw wisnae in a wheelchair,' Aggie said.

'Ah didnae say anythin' aboot a wheelchair,' the minister said, 'she was getting' pushed doon the aisle by a wee man.'

'Aye, she didnae like Harry,' Aggie said.

'At first Ah thought there was something; wrang wi' yer mother, especially when we a' witnessed her wee turn in the middle o' th aisle,' the minister said.

'She took a wee turn?' Aggie said, surprised.

'Naw, she did a wee turn – Harry Lauder. Ah think it was.' Mr McGinty's finger came up to his cheek and his eyes narrowed. 'Or was it Elvis Presley?'

Aggie's eyebrows furrowed. She had never, ever witnessed her mother doing either Harry Lauder or Elvis Presley. The Glasgow Orpheus Choir. Yes, but never the other two. She was about to query this when Mr McGinty interrupted her.

'Yer golden weddin' anniversary did ye say?'

Aggie nodded.

'So, whit hiv ye come tae me for?' he said.

'Luke 14 verses 15 tae 24,' Aggie said.

'Ah!' Mr McGinty said, nodding, 'Er that was . . . er . . . the partin' o' the Red Sea, wintit? But Ah canny help ye there, hen. Nut only can Ah no' part the Red Sea, Ah canny even part ma hair – there's nane left.'

'Naw, naw, 'Aggie said, 'it was a' aboot a man who gied a great feast and sent oot invitations tae a' his freens for tae come and get stuck intae the nosh. They a' gied excuses for no' comin' – nane o'them turned up. So, he sent his servants oot for tae bring in a' the poor and the blind and the crippled they could find – mind?'

'Ah dae, Ah dae,' Mr McGinty said. 'So, whit's that got tae dae wi' your golden weddin'? Ur you sendin' oot your servants?'

'Ah've nae servants,' Aggie said, hiding a smile.

'Ye mean for to tell me that you sent oot invitations and naebody turned up wi' a wee anniversary present for ye.'

'That's aboot it,' Aggie said, 'except ma sister Dolly. She turned up for a wee while before she went away.'

'Did she at least bring a present?' Mr McGinty asked.

'Aye, well, she – er – did bring somethin',' Aggie said.

'Whit was that, then?' the minister asked.

'A deid dug,' Aggie said.

'Aye,well, that would save ye takin' it oot walkies Ah suppose. Ye *could* take it oot slideys.' The minister sounded serious.

Aggie sighed. 'So far Ah've come across the poor and the blind but they couldnae come. Noo Ahm lookin' for the crippled,' Aggie said.

'Well!' said Mr McGinty, 'ye've come tae the right place – comin' here.'

He steered Aggie over to the window and pulled back the curtains. 'Look!' he said.

Aggie peered out and her mouth fell open. It was as though the hand of providence had guided her to this place. A group of a dozen or so people, some in wheelchairs, some with crutches were hobbling along and jostling to get into the church hall next door.

Aggie turned quizzically to Mr McGinty.

'They ur a' down-an-outs and come for get their feet seen tae,' he explained. 'Ethel is a fully qualified chiropodist and she knows her bunions. They adore her, so they dae.' Mr McGinty said with pride.

'That's very good o' her,' Aggie said.

'Aye, she's a saint,' the minister went on, 'Here's wan o' her business cards.'

Mr McGinty produced a card from a drawer and handed it to Aggie.

Aggie perused the card and a smile crossed her face, It read:

> *If ye really want a treat,*
> *come tae me and Ah'll sort yer feet.*

'That's very nice,' Aggie said.

'No'only that,' Mr McGinty said, 'efter she attends tae them, she gies them a plate o' her home made soup. They leave the hall dancin'.

'That's wonderful,' Aggie commented. 'And Ah would like for tae invite them up tae ma hoose for tae help me celebrate ma anniversary.'

'That is a good Christian attitude,' Mr McGinty said. 'C'mon intae the hall and tell them yersel'.'

Aggie followed the minister into the hall and let her eyes sweep round. Everyone sat, socks off and feet bare. The smell reminded her of a glue factory. Ethel McGinty was on her knees, a clothes peg on her nose, talking like a Dalek. Each person sighed with relief as she made her way along the rows of the corn field.

Mr McGinty stood on the platform and clapped his hands for attention. Silence followed and the wee minister cleared his throat.

'Er . . . now,' he began, 'er . . . now that yer feet has been scalped, Ah would like for to introduce youse to this wumman whose name is Aggie who has a wee treat in store for youse – Aggie.' He gestured to Aggie to join him on the platform.

'Er . . . jist a minute,' Ethel said, 'before you start.' A lady church worker had arrived with a large tureen on a trolley and the eager congregation jostled out in great expectation. They queued up orderly and happily returned to their places carrying a large bowl of Ethel's home-made broth and a chunk of crusty bread which they hungrily began to devour.

Ethel nodded to Aggie. Permission had now been given for her to continue.

'Er . . . well noo,' Aggie began, 'this is ma golden weddin' anniversary . . . ' she was interrupted by a burst of applause 'and Ah would like for youse a' tae come hame wi' me and help me celebrate.'

'A louder burst of applause greeted the news.

'Ah will phone Mr Campbell for to bring roon' his bus for tae transport youse,' Mr McGinty said.

Another round of applause accompanied by a few yells of Hurrah!

Aggie was delighted. A houseful of needy guests. Harry would

115

be playing *The Wedding Samba* with gusto on his heavenly harp if that's where he was. All Aggie needed now was to find out where Nancy was.

Mr McGinty used his mobile phone to contact Mr Campbell, who arrived within minutes. He was the great benefactor of the church and was revered as the man who had great compassion for suffering pensioners old folk who never had a visitor, never heard a kind word and who were starving and cold and living really miserable lives, who transported them on summer trips without charge. Where he took them to and did they enjoy themselves – nobody knows – for he always returned with an empty bus. It must have been a wonderful place everybody agreed, because none of the old souls ever came back.

Mr Campbell was a small skeletal looking man who wore a gestapo's peaked cap and a skull and crossbones badge on his lapel. He clapped his hands together.

'Right,' he said with a toothy smile, 'is yer feets a' done, then?'

A chorus of 'aye's went up.

'And youse ur a' goin' for a celebration nosh, that right?'

A louder chorus went up.

'Right then c'mon. Let's hiv ye,' he snapped, putting his hands together in rapid fire.

The gaiety was infectious. Aggie felt herself caught up in the happy atmosphere. She watched them troop out to the bus and gave a quick glance heavenwards and mouthed a silent thank you.

The first old lady about to step on the bus suddenly went into a convulsion and threw up, retching and heaving. She was quickly followed by the wee man behind her who sank to his knees and carpeted the pavement with Ethel's home-made soup. Every other passenger followed suit until the entire group were moaning, throwing up and holding fast their stomachs.

Mr McGinty immediately was on his mobile and, within minutes, an ambulance was screaming up. A quick examination by the paramedics who suspected that they were all suffering from food poisoning

Other ambulances, klaxons screaming screeched up and Aggie stood, mouth open, as she watched the red tail lights of the last carrier vanish round the corner and into Dalmarnock Road.

Mr McGinty saw the anguish in Aggie's eyes and put a comforting arm around her shoulder.

'Ahm sorry, hen,' he said. 'C'mon inside and Ethel'll gie ye a nice bowel o' hoat soup.'

'Er . . . naw, thanks,' Aggie said. 'Ah'll jist get up the road and see if ma daughter's arrived hame.'

Aggie walked away but a thought occurred to her. She turned back. 'Would . . . er . . . you and Ethel like for to come hame wi' me?' she said.

Mr McGinty shook his head. 'Sorry, hen,' he said, 'but Ah'd better go alang tae the Royal Infirmary an' see how ma flock is.'

Aggie said she understood and walked on, her jaw hitting the ground. This didn't happen to that bloke in the Good Book, she thought to herself.

But she was not going to be beaten. Somewhere somebody was just waiting for her invitation. She would just have to find them and hope that no calamity would befall them before she got them home.

Aggie walked down Dalmarnock Road and on to Bridgeton Cross. All was quiet underneath the Umbrella. She flopped down on a bench, leaned back and looked towards heaven.

'Where to next, God?' she murmered, adding as an afterthought, 'and if you're too busy, how aboot you, Harry. Efter a' it's your anniversary as well.'

She closed her eyes and waited for an answer.

* * *

Aggie yawned, rose and stretched herself. She was beginning to get weary of this galavanting. The good man in the Good Book would have been having palpitations by this time, she thought. She crossed over into London Road and walked slowly on towards Marquis Street where she once lived. She had many happy thoughts of the grey tenements of that street which was no longer there. Memories of hingin' oot the windae, of keeping an eye open for the rag man, of the bookie at the back of the close-mooth dashing through the backcourts as a shrill whistle from a punter alerted him to the fact that Big Tam, the polis on the beat was approaching. Of playing kick the can aleevo and beds chalked on the pavement.

117

She remembered the boys who wooed her at the back of the close. Of Wee Glaiket Geordie McFadyen whose breath stank of Wrigley's gum and who had to stand on the second step to reach her lips. Of Big Alec Anderson who tampered with tarot cards and claimed to be a fortune teller *par-excallance* and whose long nose hairs gave him the tag of *Nostril-damas*.

Aggie sighed and smiled at those days long past. She wondered what had happened to those old beaus? She had heard that Wee Glaiket had married a six-feet-two supermodel who fell madly in love with him and who put him on a pedestal. It was the only way she could get near him and Big Alec had foretold his sudden demise would occur on a day related to the number six. Being an astute fellow he avoided leaving his home on the sixth day of any month or on any date with the number six in it. He would stay in his bed, oxygen mask by his side, his phone by the bedside with the number of the minister programmed in and just waiting for the press of a button. Alas all was in vain. Alec got knocked down on the fourteenth of April by a number six bus.

Aggie sighed as the memories flooded back. She thought of her early days with Harry. He had no right to die like that and leave her alone. In a sense she blamed herself. Harry had been a bit under the weather and they had been talking about holidays and she had suggested that a Niagra trip would be a wonderful pick-me-up. After all that's where all the film stars went. But Harry had picked her up wrongly and a Viagra trip not only did not pick him up but put him down.

She thought of their younger days, Harry had his foibles and she tolerated them. They never interfered with their relationship. His weekly visits to his lodge caused some rows if she wanted to go to the Arcadia that night but it was nothing serious. Harry took his lodge visits very seriously and sometimes Aggie would get irritated when he brought it home with him. He was so staunch that he would never dial *Tim* to get the time. The very name put him off. When a priest climbed the stairs to give old Mrs O'Reilly the last rites, he climbed up at his back scooshing an aerosol disinfectant. When *Tim* was scrapped by the telephone company he hung a union jack out of the window. But Harry mellowed as the years went on and once, as the priest climbed the stairs to give

118

old Mrs O'Reilly the last rites for the umpteenth time, he even invited him in for a wee hauf. Old Mrs O'Reilly lasted until her one hundred and tenth birthday and the priest priest died at the age of forty-two of alcoholic poisoning.

Aggie wondered how this evening was going to end. The balloons in her house would be deflating just as she was. She looked heaven ward.

'Aw, Harry,' she sighed, 'whit ur ye daein' up there? It's oor anniversary, remember, son. We proamised each other that we'd celebrate it no matter whit happened. Gie's a haun' here, will ye? A sign, gie me a sign that ye're hearin' me – please. This is ma happiest night – except for the fact that you're no' here. Ye're awfu' thrawn, Harry, so ye ur. Ah decorate the hoose, put oot the invitations, suffer the smell o' curry and naebody turns up. A' the time you're up there enjoyin' yersel', playin' an' drinkin' the Harp. It's aboot time ye had yer wings clipped. C'mon noo, gies a sign.'

Aggie sighed and carried on up London Road. Suddenly she stopped dead in her tracks. The sound of an accordion playing wafted down the street. And it was playing *their* song – Harry and hers. Every couple has *their* song that romantic melody that sends them into bliss, and this was hers and Harry's. Was it a sign? Had Harry heard her and was telling her that he was there with her? Aggie's heart and pace quickened as she followed the strains of that romantic tune. Her feet and her ears led her to a vacant piece of ground. Gingerly she peered in to see where the magic music was coming from.

A few gypsy caravans were dotted around – travelling people! They were the Irish style of caravans, horse drawn and gaily coloured. A couple of horses stood tethered nearby and a woman, wearing a colourful bandanna wrapped around her head, sat on a turned up orange box by the side of a crackling camp fire. Behind her a man stood, one foot on the caravan's steps, playing the accordion. The woman caught Aggie's eye and with a wave, beckoned her to approach.

Aggie hesitated but the woman's wave became insistent and Aggie walked in to the camp site.

'Sit doon, hen,' the woman said, pushing another orange box towards her.

Aggie smiled and sat down.

'Ye're Scots, then?' she said.

'Nothin' else but,' the woman said. 'We're Scots Romany.'

'Yer music attracted me,' Aggie said. 'Is that yer man there playin' the accordion?' Aggie nodded towards the music maker.

The woman nodded. 'Aye, that's him,' she said.

'Whit's his name?' Aggie asked.

'Bam,' the gypsy said.

'Oh, is that a tradional gyspy name?' Aggie said, raising her brows.

'Naw, it's shoart for Bampot,' the woman said.

'Well, he canny hauf play that accordion,' Aggie said.

'It's a' he can dae,' the woman said.

'That song he wis playin',' Aggie went on, 'that wis ma late man and me's song. Everytime Ah hear it it takes me back tae when we wur winchin'. Ah remember we sat on board the ferry goin' doon the watter. It was a bright moonlight night and we sat under the stars and Harry held ma haun' and an accordion player played that song and Harry, squeezing' ma haun' sang it tae me. It was dead romatic, so it wis.'

'And where is he – Harry the night?' the woman asked.

'He's deid,' Aggie said, dabbing her eye.

'Aw, whit a shame,' the gypsy woman commiserated.

'An' it's oor golden weddin' anniversary,' Aggie went on as though rubbing salt in the wound.

'Aw!' the woman said, then, turning to her husband, yelled, 'Hey, Bam, c'mere you.'

The man shuffled over. 'Whit is it?' he said gruffily.

'That wumman's man's deid and that wis their song you was playin'.'

'So, dae ye want me for tae resurrect him or somethin'?' Bam snapped.

'It's their golden weddin' – so whit aboot it?'

'Whit aboot whit?' Bam said.

Aggie tugged his sleeve, 'Play it again, Bam,' she said dabbing her eye.

Bam adjusted the straps of his accordion and began to play *Donald Where's yer Troosers?*

Aggie dreamily found herself singing the words . . . *'Ah've jist came down from the Isle of Skye . . . '*

Yes, Harry had heard her and had let her know that he had heard her. How else could that gypsy know to play *their* song – *Donald Where's yer Troosers?*

Aggie savoured every note as Bam played on. She was transported back to that ferry on the romantic night. Harry had sung just for her. Many people had said that he had a voice like Robert Wilson – or was it Harold Wilson? Aggie couldn't remember. But it didn't matter, it was music to her ears.

As he finished the song Bam held out his hand and Aggie rummaged in her bag and placed a fifty-pence piece in his hand. Bam pocketed the coin and ambled away muttering.

'That was lovely!' Aggie said.

'Aye, songs can dae that tae ye,' the woman said. 'Bam studied under Jimmy Shand,' she added.

'Jimmy Shand taught him tae play the accordion?' Aggie gasped.

'Naw, Bam lived in the hoose under him,' the woman said. 'Noo,' she went on, 'would ye like for me tae tell you yer fortune?'

'Ah've got nae future,' Aggie said sadly.

'Nonesense!' the gypsy said. 'Jist cross ma palm wi' paper.'

'Ye mean silver. Don't ye?' Aggie said.

'Inflation,' the woman said.

Aggie produced a one pound note and thrust it into the woman's hand.

The gypsy screwed up her nose but said nothing. She examined Aggie's hand and Aggie was startled to see her brows furrowing.

'Whit is it . . . whit is it?' she said worriedly.

'You ur gonny be accosted by a foreign man wearing a balaclava who will mug you for your handbag.'

'Ah'll clobber him wi' it,' Aggie said determinedly.

'Jist be careful, hen,' the gypsy said.

'Ah wull,' Aggie nodded. 'And, seein' youse hiv been that good tae me playin' oor song an' that how would youse like for tae come ham wi' me an' help me celebrate ma anniversary?'

'Aw, thanks a lot, hen,' the woman said. 'If there's grub there you don't hiv tae ask twice.'

Aggie was elated. Harry had surely heard her plea. The gypsy woman stood up.

'Bam,' she yelled, 'Tell everybody we ur invited oot tae dinner.'

'Everybody?' Aggie wondered how many travelling folk there would be. Reading her thoughts, the woman laughed.

'There's twenty-four of us,' she said.

'Don't bring the hoarses,' Aggie said. At last she was happy. She would have a full house, Bam could play his accordion and to hell with her neighbour from hell. Within seconds the complete tribe had gathered in front of their generous hostess.

'Ah want for to thanks youse for accepting ma invitation,' Aggie said. 'Youse hiv made ma day. Noo a' Ah hiv tae worry aboot is findin' ma lassie, Nancy and things would really be hunky-dorey. Noo, if youse would jist follow me.'

A cry of joy went up from the gathered crowd and they were about to follow Aggie out of the vacant lot when three police cars and a van screamed to a halt barring their way. A senior officer and a dozen or so men spilled out. The officer with the scrambled eggs on his hat threw open wide his arms.

'Right, you lot,' he snapped, 'youse were ordered for to leave this site by twelve hunner hours today. And youse have nut moved wan inch. So, unless youse want for to spend the night in the cells and come before the magistrate the morra, Ah am givin' youse this wan last chance for to move on – at wance.'

He emphasised the last part. The travellers mumbled and shuffled their feet and turned about.

'Sorry, hen,' the woman with the bandanna said, 'this is an occupational hazzard – but thanks jist the same.'

Horses were quickly harnessed and a sad Aggie watched as the campers moved out – another disappointment. It was as though Auld Nick himself was out to scupper her big night.

Aggie watched and heard the clippety-clop of the horses and the rumble of the wagons head out of town. A red lantern hung on the back of the last caravan and swayed gently. She watched as the light grew dimmer in the distance and was about to turn away when the sound of accordion music floated up in the evening air.

Donald Where's yer Troosers whisked her once more to that ferry which was steaming doon the watter. Not only was the ferry steaming, Harry, too, was steaming. She was back on that deck where she sat so many years ago. The red light vanished completely as Aggie walked on.

With a shudder, she suddenly thought of that gypsy woman's frightening prediction that a foreign man wearing a balaclava would accost her for her handbag.

Aggie gritted her teeth which she was glad she had put in that night and walked on up London Road. Her eyes darted from left to right and back again from right to left.

It happened in a flash. One minute nobody was there and the next he stood directly in front of her. She would have gritted her teeth still further but was afraid she would break them.

'Right, Frau, gie's un bag.'

'Away an' bile yer heid,' Aggie snapped, clutching her bag tightly into herself.

'Vot?' the man snarled.

Aggie took a step back and surveyed her accoster. The gypsy was right. He was small, had a foreign accent and wore a balaclava. He wasn't too old either. There was something about him that Aggie recognised. She could not see his face – but that accent? Not many Germans lived in Bridgeton. The man took a step closer and Aggie took a step backwards.

'I don't vant for to hurt you, frau,' he said, at the same time raising his fist, 'but I vont your bag.'

Suddenly that voice clicked. Aggie knew at once who this upstart was. 'Ah know who you ur,' Aggie said with a defiant rasp.

'Naw, you don't,' the attacker said.

'Oh aye Ah dae,' Aggie was adamant.'Yer accent gave ye away.'

'Ah haff not got un accent,' the man said with frustration.

'Un has,' Aggie said. 'You ur Daftie Von McFadyen, grandson of Wee Glaikit George McFayden, who married a ten-fit tall supermodel and emigrated tae Germany where he lived in a ten-roomed red-brick mansion in Munich, that had wance belanged tae Adolph Hitler – that's who un is.'

'Shut up!' the balaclava bandit snapped. 'Zis is a luger I haff in my mitt.'

'Been drinkin', eh?' Aggie said, nonchalantly, 'ma Harry drank ten o' them a day.'

'*Luger*,' the man screamed, 'nein *lager!*'

'Luger, smoogar,' Aggie sneered, 'ye're still Daftie McFadyen.'

'I am nein Daftie McFadyen,' the man bawled and sounding hysterical, 'I am Heinrich Von Richter, a famous pilot of the vunerbar Focke-Volf.'

'Ye don't need tae swear,' Aggie snapped.

'Nein swearing,' the man snapped, 'Ze Focke-Volf is ze greatest fighter plane in ze vorld.'

'Ye're that famous then that ye left yer ten-mansioned hoose that belanged tae Adolph Hitler an' decided for tae move intae a wee single-end in Brigton? No' only that, ye set oot tae mug an auld aged pensioner in London Road? An' no' only that you wull nut admit that you ur wee Daftie McFadyen.'

The man went into a rage and stamped his foot. 'I am nut Daftie McFadyen,' he screamed. 'I am Erich Von Richter, ze famous . . . '

He did not finish the sentence. His mobile phone rang and, angrily, he pulled it from his pocket.

'Hello,' he bawled, 'Ja, zis is Daftie McFadyen . . . nein. I am busy robbing un old frau'. Ja, see you at ze torture club. Aufwiedersehn.'

'Ah-Ha,' Aggie said as he tucked the phone into his pocket, 'Daftie right enough. You ur Daftie McFadyen, nae doot aboot it.'

'Zat vas a mistook in ma part,' he said, kicking himself. 'So, ze bag, at vonce – or else.' He waved the gun under her nose.

'Look,' Aggie said, 'yer wee grandfaither was no' a bad wee man – glaikit but no' bad. He would turn in his urn if he knew whit you wur daein', so he would.'

The mugger shuffled his feet and stared at the ground. 'You knew ma gan'papa, eh?' he said.

'Ah could've been yer granny,' Aggie said.

'Ya make me ashamed,' he said.

'And so ye should be,' Aggie said, 'robbin' auld wimmen when ye should be daein' a hard day's work. Whit dae ye expect tae get oot an auld wumman's bag. Eh? Her bus pass? Her pension book? Her photay o' Daniel O'Donnel?'

Daftie was getting frustrated at the stand this old woman was taking. His victims were always instantly submissive.

'The bag,' he snarled.

Aggie swung the bag as hard as she could and walloped him across his face.

'It's a good skelpin ye need,' she said.

Daftie McFadyen's hand came up to his face and slipping it under his balaclava, he rubbed his cheek furiously. Then he raised his hand as though to strike Aggie.

'Don't you dare,' she yelled.

The mugger's hand froze when he saw a couple of men yelling and running towards him.

Grabbing Aggie's bag, he dashed across London Road to make his escape. Old women he could handle but not a couple of Bridgeton men.

Aggie yelled *thief* at the top of her voice. The tyres of the number sixty-four bus screamed as the horrified driver slammed on his brakes. Daftie McFadyen screamed too as the vehicle slammed into him, sending him ten feet into the air and crashing him to the ground.

Aggie's hand came up to her mouth. 'Oh, my God!' she gasped and hurried over to retrieve her bag. Daftie lay groaning on the ground and suddenly Aggie felt sorry for him. Having taken lessons on First Aid in her younger days she knelt down and ran her hands over his body.

She pulled off his balaclava. Yes, he was Wee Glaikit's kin all right. That same bulbous nose – with two warts. Daftie had that same affliction.

After examining her would-be attacker Aggie would not, for the sake of Daftie's grandfather, mention that he was about to mug her or snatch her bag.

'Ye're gonny be a'right, son,' she said. 'Ye've jist got two broken legs, a fractured erm an' yer teeth wur rotten anyway.'

'Danke, Frau,' Daftie spluttered, spitting out was was left of his teeth.

'Wid ye like tae come tae a party, son?' Aggie said.

Daftie did not answer. An ambulance had arrived and the paramedics were attending to him.

Aggie stood up and sighed as the ambulance, sirens wailing, raced away towards the Royal Infirmary.

Aggie's anniversary plans were a disaster. Nothing had gone right and she wondered why. Harry hadn't been as cooperative as he might have been. He was probably flirting around with some wee angel up there. Aggie would clip his wings when she next saw him. Gritting her teeth she suddenly couldn't wait to snuff it, Brigton had changed since the old days and she noted just how much as she walked on up London Road. It was like being in another city altogether. But she still had her wonderful memories. She could smell the flying cinders from a thousand billowing chimney tops, could hear the gravel bellow of the coalman, the clatter of zinc milk urns shifting about on board a rickety cart. All was changed now. Those sights and sounds had vanished and some would say good riddance.

Now, passing a line of super modern houses with manicured little gardens, she remembered how a greengrocer's shop was once on that site. Old Jack Wilson sold everything from carrots to carnations. It was from Wilson's little greengrocer's shop, on each anniversary, that Harry would purchase a single red rose and march into the house. His chest puffed out he proudly fastened it on her hair, followed by a kiss. If he was flush she might get a bunch of daffodils. But nothing smelled sweeter in this world than that single red rose.

The snow had eased up but Aggie still felt the chill of the night. It had been a frosty night in more ways than one. She worried about Nancy. What had happened to her? Was Wee Alice's stalker a crazed mugger or even worse? She had visions of them both lying bloodied in some dark alleyway. Aggie shuddered and pulled her collar more tightly around her neck.

She decided that the man in the Good Book had better luck than she had and decided to head for home. Besides, the chill was beginning to gnaw at her bones and there was a hope that Nancy might have phoned – assuming that she was fully erect and un-injured and had an explanation for her disappearence. Well, it *was* a hope although Aggie had by now convinced herself that a new Jack the Ripper was on the prowl in Brigton. Aggie's steps quickened and, approaching her corner she hoped that, as she turned round the bend, she would see her house ablaze with light – meaning that Nancy was in and was safe. But the house was in total darkness as she turned the corner. Aggie's heart sank. She didn't really expect to see lights from her windows but she had said a silent prayer.

Aggie hurried up the pathway and, with shaking hand inserted the key in the door. She felt the welcoming warmth of the house the minute she stepped in the door. Quickly. She tore off her coat and hung it over the hall stand. Hurrying into the kitchen she wasted no time in putting the kettle on the hob. A good cup of hot, sweet tea would soon thaw her out, she thought. She next entered the living room and lifted the phone. Nancy just may have been trying to contact her. She dialled one four seven one, where the telephone operator informs of the last number dialled to your telephone. No, the number given by the operator was the number for Esther earlier on. So only silence from Nancy. That was more worry for Aggie. The screaming whistle of the kettle sent her hurrying back into the kitchen. Aggie brewed up a hot cup of tea, took a biscuit from the cookie jar and returned to the living room. Placing the tea on the table top, Aggie switched the radio on and her eyes fell on Harry's photo on top of the sideboard. She sighed as DJ David Jacobs played Frank Sinatra singing the Cole Porter classic, *I've got you Under My Skin*. She pressed the picture to her heart and flopped on to the easy chair by the dining table.

Aggie closed her eyes for a moment and savoured the music.

'*Aggie!*' the voice startled her and she sat bolt upright.

'*Aggie!*' the voice repeated. Aggie jumped to her feet.

Harry, bathed in dazzling light, stood in the corner of the room, his arms outstretched.

'Tha . . . tha . . . that you, Harry?' Aggie stammered.

'Aye, it's me, sweetheart,' Harry said, coming closer.

Aggie felt her legs buckling but Harry's strong arms held her. 'Happy Anniversary, hen,' he said.

'Bu . . . bu . . . ' Aggie began.

'Nae buts, hen,' Harry said, 'Ah telt ye we'd celebrate this golden day.'

Sinatra ended his song and the Glenn Miller Orchestra began to play *The Anniversary Waltz*.

'Ah'll bet you fixed this,' Aggie smiled, holding him tightly.

Harry smiled knowingly and they danced around the floor.

Aggie was in dream land and Harry guided her back to the easy chair and kissed her lightly on the forehead.

Aggie closed her eyes dreamily only to open them quickly at the persistent knocking at the door. She jumped up. Harry was nowhere to be seen. It had been a dream – a wonderful, marvellous dream. She smiled. She didn't care. It was real to her. For one brief moment her wedding celebration was as it should have been. Knowing Harry he had probably conned God into giving him a few moments leave. Or maybe it was the other way. Maybe God felt sorry for her – all her trekking around, like His Good Book said, her disappointment.

'Away doon there, Harry,' He had said, 'an' gie Aggie a wee bit comfort.'

Yes, He knows. Aggie hurried to the door. The big policeman who had taken Sammy away stood on the doorstep. Aggie's jaw dropped.

'Oh, naw!' she gasped, 'It's Nancy, int it!' Visions of Nancy lying bludgeoned and lifeless flooded her mind.

The policeman nodded. 'Aye, we've found her and her wee pal, Alice.'

'Wh . . . where?' Aggie stuttered.

'C'mon, we'll take ye tae them,' the policeman said.

Aggie grabbed her coat from the hall stand and hurriedly followed the policeman out to the waiting police car with its blue lights flashing. The car sped off, sirens wailing heading down London Road screaming towards the city.

Aggie, sitting in the back, was shaking. 'Ah knew it, Ah knew it,' she kept repeating to herself. Tearfully, she leaned forward and asked, 'How is she?'

The big cop said nothing.

'Where is she?' Aggie pleaded.

'The Royal,' he said, without turning round.

This only made Aggie wail even louder, 'and whit aboot wee Alice?'

'She's wi' her,' the policeman said.

The police car raced on – until it came to Abercromby Street where it veered right and speeded up towards Duke Street, and took a sharp left and hurried along towards John Knox Street, where it turned. Aggie was at the edge of her seat.

'Ur they bad?' she nearly choked on the last word.

'Ye'll see yerel',' the cop said.

As the car turned the bend the mighty Glasgow Cathedral came into view and adjacent to it, the huge imposing building of the Royal Infirmary. Aggie closed her eyes tightly. All thoughts of her scuppered anniversary celebration had now gone. There was a deeper depression now. Poor Nancy and Wee Alice! She waited for the feel of the car to swing right and go through the large iron gate of the hospital but, instead. She felt the sway of the car turn *left*.

Quickly, she opened her eyes. The car had swung into Cathedral Street and was racing along, sirens still wailing. Aggie turned and looked out of the back window. The Royal was quickly receding from view. The car suddenly turned right into North Hanover Street and then left into Killermont Street, screaming to a stop outside a large sandy-stone building.

'Whit's this?' Aggie asked, puzzled. 'Ye said Nancy was in the Royal.'

'And so she is,' the big cop said, '*The Royal Concert Hall.*' Smiling, he stepped out of the car and opened the back door. Taking Aggie by the hand, he helped her alight, puzzlement in her eyes. Escorting her inside, he squeezed her hand. 'There ye are, safe an' sound,' he said.

'*Mammy!*' the voice made Aggie turn. Her eyes widened as Nancy hurried towards her.

'*Nancy,*' Aggie yelled joyously sweeping her daughter into her arms, 'and ye're a'right.'

'Of coorse Ah'm a'right. Mammy,' Nancy said. 'Ah'm here tae pick up tickets for the Johnnie Beattie and Alexander Brothers show next week when they're daein' a tribute tae Andy Stewart – you know, don't ye? *Donald Where's yer troosers.*'

Aggie sighed. 'Oh. Aye, Ah know, But why drag me away oot here. Ye could've phoned. Ah was worried sick.'

'Ah dragged ye away oot here because,' Nancy hesitated, 'Ach, c'mon, you're comin' wi' me.'

Taking her mother by the hand, Nancy led her out of the

building and across the road in the recently built Langs Hotel. They entered through a huge door – into darkness.

'Whit's this?' Aggie heard herself say. As though a signal had been given, the room became a blaze of light. And a band struck up *Congratulations*.

'Happy anniversary, Mammy.' Nancy said, pecking her cheek. 'Ah telt ye Ah was savin' up. But it wisnae for ma engagement it was for this a' alang. Ah couldnae tell ye – everybody was in the secret.'

A Crescendo of welcome almost blew the roof off. Aggie's happy eyes scanned the huge, applauding and rapturous crowd. Everyone was there, Wee Alice, Esther, Dolly, Chu Chu, Sammy, the big polis and even the Lord Provost himself, wearing his chain of office.

'Sammy hisnae been charged efter a',' Nancy said. 'The Lord Provost said it was a case of mistaken identity. In fact Sammy might even get a reward for finding' the loast chain.'

Aggie laughed and dabbed her eyes. Aye, oor Sammy would she thought.

Aggie was led into the middle of the floor and the cheering guests gathered in a circle around her. Everybody sang *Auld Lang Syne* and followed it with *Donald Where's yer Troosers*.

Soon everyone was dancing, gaily coloured balloons dropped from the ceiling and the place rocked with happy laughter.

* * *

'Right, c'mon Mammy,' Nancy said as Aggie staggered a little. 'Time you were hame tae yer bed.'

Aggie smiled. It *had* been a hectic day. She turned at the door and waved as silence descended.

'Ah want tae thank youse all for makin' this the happiest night in ma life – except for Harry an' ma weddin' night, that is. Ah'm jist sorry he wisnae here . . . but then, he wisnae really a' there that night either.'

A ring of laughter echoed round the room.

'Ah thought a' ma freens had deserted me. But youse have made me proud – thanks a million.'

A cheer went up and Aggie blew a kiss to the assembly. Nancy took her mother's arm and led her out into the chill of night. A white stretch limo sat outside. The uniformed chauffeur opened wide the door, Aggie and Nancy climbed in and flopped down.

'Phew! Ah'm exhausted!' Aggie sighed. 'Thanks, hen – for everything,' she said, pecking Nancy's cheek.

Nancy squeezed her mother's arm affectionately. They arrived home in no time.

'Like a cuppa tea, Mammy?' Nancy asked.

'Naw, Ah think Ahll jist get tae ma bed,' Aggie said, adding, 'although Ah don't know if Ah'll sleep.'

They said their Good nights and Aggie made her way into her bedroom. She sat at the edge of the bed, her mind racing.

'Aye, it was quite a night,' she thought to herself.

She stood up, stretched and her eyes fell on her pillow. Resting there was a single red rose. She took it up and holding it closely, let it brush against her cheek enjoying its fragrance. She kissed it and smiled.

'Oh Harry,' she whispered, 'ye're an awfu' man!'.

LINDSAY PUBLICATIONS
PO BOX 812 GLASGOW G14 9NP
TEL/FAX 0141 569 6060
ISBN Prefix 1 898169

1 898169 29 2	They Rose Again	£12.99
28 4	Nippon Aboot	£4.99
27 6	The Cardinal	£9.99
26 8	Full Cycle	£9.99
20 9	Topsy & Tim agus na Smaladairean	£4.99
19 5	Topsy & Tim aig an Dotair	£4.99
25 X	Oor Hoose	£4.99
21 7	Topsy & Tim agus na Poilis	£4.99
18 7	Topsy & Tim aig an Fhiaclair	£4.99
22 5	Laughing Matters	£8.99
24 1	Oot the Windae	£7.99
23 3	A Wheen O' Blethers	£8.99
17 9	Will I be Called an Author?	£7.99
16 0	Away with the Ferries	£9.99
15 2	Twisted Knickers & Stolen Scones	£9.99
14 4	Happy Landings	£4.99
11 X	Lines Around the City	£10.99
13 6	Still a Bigot	£4.99
12 8	Savour of Scotland	£5.99
10 1	The Surgeon's Apprentice	£4.99
03 0	Scottish Home Cooking	£4.95
05 5	A Taste of Scotland	£8.99
06 3	Homecraft: The Dundee Cookbook	£3.99
07 1	Robert Burns: Scotland's National Poet	£4.99
08 X	Glasgow's River	£9.99
01 2	Highland Dancing 6th EDN	£10.00
30 6	Aggie's Anniversary	£5.99